DATE DUE

EVERYTHING
THEY EVER
WANTED

EVERYTHING THEY EVER WANTED

•

Carol Blake Gerrond

AVALON BOOKS
THOMAS BOUREGY AND COMPANY, INC.
401 LAFAYETTE STREET
NEW YORK, NEW YORK 10003

PRINTED IN THE UNITED STATES OF AMERICA
ON ACID-FREE PAPER
BY HADDON CRAFTSMEN, BLOOMSBURG, PENNSYLVANIA

To Roxanne Stone and Ed Safiran, Jr.
Your advice was indispensable!

Chapter One

Mollie Moreau grinned, pushing back the lock of wine-red hair whipping against her face. "I hope they don't still burn people for witchcraft in this part of Illinois!"

Her red Ford pickup boiled around another curve in the roller-coaster back road, thick dust and young laughter pluming in its wake.

Passenger DeeAnn Jones leaned toward Mollie. "What brought that on?"

"You didn't hear the grilling I got just now at the grocery store?"

DeeAnn shook her head no.

"Well! The clerk looks at the check, then goes, *'Indian Prairie Farm?* That the . . . *camp* they're setting up on the old Riley place?' Just the way she said 'camp'—kind of snidelike." Mollie shook her head. "She meant *cult*. Weird cult."

Dee giggled. "I suppose you spoiled her fun, told her Indian Prairie will be just a plain, innocent vacation farm?"

"Sure. For what good it did. She stares at me over the top of her glasses, very suspicious, then says, 'Whatever!' "

Mollie's laughter stopped short. In the rearview mirror, an object was coming up through the murk behind the truck—fast!

1

''Hold on, Dee!'' Mollie pulled the Ford hard right, slashing into the pebbly road shoulder.

A brazen roar, a blast of gravel—and an old Harley-Davidson swooped up beside the truck, steadied long enough for Mollie to get a glimpse of white teeth and flying black hair, then barreled past up the road ahead.

''Holy cats!'' Mollie exploded. ''A road about four feet wide, a hill *and* a curve—and Evel Knievel passes?''

Dee peered after the speed demon. ''Mollie, wasn't that the biker tough who pulled in at the Shawano gas station just as we were leaving?'' She shook her head. ''No jacket, no helmet—that handsome dude's just begging to be hamburger.''

''Handsome?'' Mollie scoffed. ''The way he swung that piece of tin up to the gas pump, I didn't give him a second glance.''

No. But a first glance had told her: The tough was also a hunk.

Mollie slowed the Ford to a bumpy standstill as both young women madly cranked windows against the choking grit billowing through the cab.

Dee's sturdy frame rocked with a huge sneeze. ''That's not the repairman—'' She clamped a tissue to her nose to ward off a second eruption. ''—your aunt is sending to fix up the guesthouse, is it?''

Mollie's chuckle was brief and dry. ''George Kincannon? No way! George is an old guy—at least fifty. And his idea of a cool ride is his Mr. Fixit panel truck.''

''Good. 'Cause I wouldn't put much faith in anybody crazy enough to pass *us* like we were standing still.'' Dee held up a hand. ''Look—white knuckles!''

''Whoa, now!'' Mollie protested through a sheepish

grin. "You're still a city girl, Dee. When you've lived out here longer, ten miles from anywhere, you'll push it, too."

Dee laughed. "You sound like my husband, Ray. All you born 'n' bred country kids are just cowboys behind the wheel."

"Yee-hah!" Mollie chortled.

The air was beginning to clear. Mollie put the Ford back on the road, though not so fast as before. More chat and laughter, another mile, and then a sign reading *Indian Prairie Farm*. Mollie turned down a long, narrow lane. The bright May sun shone on lush wild grasses to the left, a horse pasture centered by a large pond on the right. Mollie pulled into a farmyard beside an old two-story house covered in dirt-gray shingles.

That is, part of the house was dirt-gray. Additions, including a flat-roofed afterthought sided in yellow vinyl, sprouted like warts off the main structure. The long front porch was topped by a green fiberglass roof. From the front doorknob hung a forlorn wreath of cornhusks and faded plastic flowers.

For a second, the young women sat silent, contemplating the view.

"Doesn't it kinda—intimidate you, Mollie?" Dee ventured. "I mean, this place is going to take *work*."

Mollie shook her head no. "Dee, for two years I was an insurance adjuster—in *Chicago*. Believe me, I'm excited, not scared. *This* will be a dream job!"

They alighted from the truck. "Besides," Mollie went on as they retrieved boxes of supplies from the truck bed, "I'll have good help, between you and George Kincannon. You can cook anything, and George can repair anything."

Dee started toward the house, then turned. "Mollie,

Ray and I have been talking: Since we live just down the road, maybe you'd like to sleep over with us till the farm opens.''

Mollie smiled. ''You've been married—what, six months? You don't need company.''

''But what if that motorcycle geek—or someone like him—comes around? You got a gun?''

''Nope. I'm more scared of guns than I am of geeks.''

They headed around a corner of the house, toward the back door. ''Besides,'' Mollie said, ''he's probably flying low over the state line by now—''

''Hi.''

Mollie nearly dropped the grocery box.

An old Harley-Davidson stood parked under a tree. Against it leaned a tall young man in black jeans and T-shirt. His coal-black hair streamed to his shoulders from under a baseball cap, worn backward. He flashed a white, cocky smile.

''Remember me?'' His voice was deep and relaxed, but the accent suggested Chicago. Mean Streets, Chicago.

Mollie set down her burden. It had been twelve years. He'd grown up. But the tanned, high cheekbones, the eyes—brown to the point of black and full of challenge—now that she looked straight into them . . .

''I remember.'' She didn't sound pleased.

His charcoal eyes took in all of her—her plain denim shirt and no-name jeans; thick burgundy hair falling out of a loose French braid. And those unusual eyes. Turquoise with just a hint of tilt. Some people had said Mollie's eyes were gorgeous. But once this man had called them ''cat eyes.''

Oh, yes. She remembered Zachary Kincannon, all right. Only twelve years ago, he'd been half a head shorter—and a whole lot more ornery—than she was. It still jolted her, the misery he'd caused her that preteen summer she'd stayed in Chicago with her aunt Gwen Harris. Every time George Kincannon came to do repair work at the Harrises', he'd brought along his beastly little son, Zach. Taunts, tricks, anything to remind Mollie that she was a klutzy farm girl, not a slick city chick—Zach had used them all.

"Yeah, I vaguely recall you, Zach," she said coolly. "Weren't you the guy I punched out for calling me 'Red,' and 'farm girl'?"

He laughed easily. Nonchalantly. "You could do it then." He stood straight and casually stretched a hard-muscled frame. He must have been six feet three or four. "I don't think it'd work now. Do you?"

There it was—the same flip attitude, the same taunting dare in his dark eyes that used to make Mollie fly off the handle and hammer him.

"You keep tearing that Harley over these loose gravel roads, and there won't be enough left of you for me to smack."

He looked down at her with cool amusement. "You care? Back at that gas station, you snooted me like I was already some kind of roadkill."

"Really? I don't remember even *looking* at you!"

"Uh—ahem!"

Mollie had forgotten Dee was still standing there clutching a heavy box.

"Want some help?" Zach strolled over to Dee and took the box from her arms. "My name's Zach Kincannon."

"Oh—uh—" Dee stammered. She brushed a hand

through her short blond hair. "I'm—DeeAnn Jones. 'Dee' for short. I'll be housekeeper and cook here at the farm, once the place opens. In the meantime, I'm helping Mollie get things ready."

Zach nodded. "Welcome to the club. My peon days start tomorrow."

"*Wha-a-at?*"

Zach's smile widened at Mollie's squawk. "Didn't your aunt tell you? I'm gonna work here, too."

"You? What are *you* supposed to do?"

Zach glanced around at the unpromising surroundings. A hundred feet from the dismal main house, a small dwelling once earmarked for the hired man's use crouched in humble disrepair. A corncrib, a small garage, and a toolshed, all in need of help—lots of it—and a horse barn completed the outbuildings. Only the horse barn looked sturdy enough to withstand more than a light breeze.

Zach's brow hiked. "Not much." He nodded toward the house. "Just get this heap livable by the end of the month." He chuckled at Mollie's sharp gasp. "Who put this mess together? Shemp, Curly, and Moe?"

Mollie glared. "Your dad can make things right. *He's* the one we're counting on."

Zach snorted. "Ha! The old man came down here for a look-see a couple of weeks ago, just before you got here. And bailed out. Said it'd take a better man than he is to get this joint jumpin' by June first."

Let this be a bad dream! Mollie prayed. *Let it be gone by morning!*

He grinned, and Mollie could see how much he still enjoyed rattling her. "So," he said to Dee, "lead the way into Hotel Herman Munster."

Mollie smothered a few choice words. Then she picked up her own box of supplies and followed into the house.

Zach looked around the big kitchen. A cocked brow replaced his derisive grin. He set the box he was carrying on the chrome dinette table. "I know this is supposed to be for guests of humble circumstance, but isn't this kinda pushin' the envelope?" He turned those mocking dark eyes on Mollie. "I mean—who's gonna *pay* to stay here?"

Okay. Dingy white metal cabinets and a huge, old-fashioned white sink, chipped here and there down to the cast iron; countertops and floor of matching dull tan linoleum; a hard-used electric stove and an antique refrigerator: 1940 revisited. Mollie conceded a point.

Zach's thumbs hooked on his jeans pockets. "You sure Henry Harris wasn't on a toot when he bought this?"

Mollie flared at the remark. "Uncle Henry made a fortune in real estate! He knew what he was doing!"

Zach laughed. "Sure he did—most of the time. But buying a bunch of hills and grass, and a house hit by the ugly stick—all so he could start some kind of retreat for stressed-out Chicagoans—you gotta wonder."

"I don't wonder at all!" Mollie claimed.

Actually, she did wonder. Had from the first moment she'd heard that Uncle Henry, just before his sudden death a few months ago, had bought nine hundred acres of Illinois woods, water, and prairie with the intention of turning it into a simple, affordable vacation farm. But she wasn't going to satisfy Zach Kincannon's overgrown ego by admitting it.

Zach shrugged. "I'll get the rest of your stuff," he said to Dee.

The second he was out of sight, Dee turned to Mollie. "Have we got a problem here?" she said hesitantly.

Mollie groaned and dropped her burden on the tabletop. "I can't believe Aunt Gwen would do this to me! She knows I can't stand Zach Kincannon! Didn't she have to separate us enough times when I stayed with her and Uncle Henry? Before I beat the tar out of Zach, that is."

"Well, like the guy says, I wouldn't try that now," Dee whispered. "Man! Did you get a load of those delts and pecs?"

Mollie sneered. "Don't get taken in by the Body by Soloflex. Underneath is a rude, crude jerk—"

Dee developed a lightning-fast interest in unloading groceries.

Zach sauntered slowly from the doorway. Mollie jumped as he dropped the last big box dangerously close to her feet. His eyes had gone jet-black. She was aware that a very tough man—a very angry man—stood within inches of her.

"Here's the rest of your supplies, *ma'am*," he grated. "Mind if I take a seat, *ma'am*, or should I just go out to my straw pile in the horse barn—*ma'am*?"

Without waiting for an answer, he swung a chair from the table and straddled it. His fierce glare never let go of Mollie's equally ireful gaze.

"Don't wear yourself out on effects, Zach. I don't think you'll be here long enough to need lodging."

His sinewy arms folded across the back of the chair. A grim smile tugged at his lips. "What makes you think so, Miss Mollie, *ma'am*?"

"Because I'm un-hiring you right now."

He laughed outright. Unpleasantly. "Sorry. You're not my boss. Gwen Harris is."

Mollie snapped, "Aunt Gwen put me in charge here! I hire, I fire!"

"Pick up the phone. Call her. See what she says."

His utter confidence shook Mollie. She'd never known Zach to be a liar.

"I'll—call her later," she muttered. "I have some other things—important things—to discuss with her."

Zach's jaw thrust aslant. "Good. In the meantime, I haven't eaten all day. Got anything I could chow down on?"

Mollie jumped at the chance to vex him. She pointed to a bag of groceries. "Sorry. The Indian Prairie kitchen isn't open yet. You'll have to fend for yourself."

The skin darkened even more under Zach's cheekbones. He glared at Mollie for a second, then made a sudden lunge at the nearest bag. He grabbed a loaf of French bread, tore off the wrapper, and sank his teeth into a huge chunk. "Sorry to offend your tender sensibilities, *ma'am*," he spluttered through a hail of bread crumbs, "but us rude, crude jerks don't have no manners, no how!"

Mollie roiled with anger.

Dee was a big help. She burst out laughing. At Mollie's baleful stare, she stifled. "Uh . . . I think it's time for me to go home and fix Raymond's supper. See you tomorrow, Mollie." She was out of there.

Zach swallowed his wad of bread. Then he wiped the crumbs from his mouth and laid the remainder of the loaf on the table. He rose slowly from his chair.

"Thank you for your hospitality, *ma'am*. I sure appreciate it, *ma'am*."

"Will you stop with the 'ma'ams'?" Mollie scathed. "I'm not your drill sergeant."

"Hey, baby—" He stepped closer, towering over her modest height. "Haven't you always felt like you're a queen bee? And I'm a lowly drone?"

"I've always felt like you've gone out of your way to make fun of me."

"If I have, it's because you're such a good target. Always all pumped up, aren't you? Just like Auntie Gwen. Smarter, tougher, bossier than anyone else." A rough chuckle broke his frown; he relaxed, leaning against the chair back. "If your opinion of yourself was any higher, you'd need a stepladder to reach it!"

"Why, you—you—you Harley-riding street boy! No wonder you don't wear a bike helmet—your head is too big!"

Zach's slow, self-possessed grin maddened Mollie. His long fingers flicked a crumb of French bread off the table, toward her. "Chill, baby. I'm gonna stow my sleeping bag in the barn and start figuring out what I can do to save this dump. Call me when dinner's ready."

"Call you—!" Mollie sputtered. He was already walking out the door. "You'll starve first!" she yelled at his receding back.

" 'Call me when dinner's ready'!" she repeated to the empty room. "Of all the nerve! I'm going put in a call, all right! To Aunt Gwen. She's got some explaining to do!"

Chapter Two

"That macho jerk!"

Zach's breezy dinner order still rankled as Mollie stomped out to the horse barn for the late afternoon feeding. Ordinarily she looked forward to this chance to bond with her new trail herd while they nickered and snorted over their corn and oats mixed with molasses. She'd always gotten a kick out of the way horses, with teeth strong enough to sever an unwary finger, delicately mumbled grain around a feedbox.

But this afternoon she was not amused. One of the conditions of managing Indian Prairie was that she would be giving orders, not taking them. Mollie liked that. A lot. So she was still seething as she patted thirteen noses and scratched twenty-six ears. "I'll call 'im for supper," she muttered. "I've got just the menu for him—hot tongue and cold shoulder!"

She was still grumbling later as she gave up trying to reach Aunt Gwen at home and tried her car phone number. Mollie's immediate request to fire Zach met an equally immediate "No!"

"Aunt Gwen, you know I can't stand Zachary Kincannon. Why didn't you tell me you were sending him to take his father's place?"

Aunt Gwen's usually silky tones had a little edge. "I'm living with a lot of pressures nowadays, Mollie. Surely you can understand that."

Mollie felt a tug of sympathy. Her tone softened. "Of course you are, Aunt Gwen. But I thought I was hired to be manager of Indian Prairie. Not share authority with—with—that jerk!"

"See what I mean? Name-calling already. If I'd told you he was coming, you'd have walked. And now that you've persuaded me to turn Indian Prairie over to you, I need you to make it work."

The subtle reminder of just who had originated the idea of Mollie Moreau, Manager, wasn't lost on Mollie. Still, she persisted. "Aunt Gwen, I can hire someone local to do the repairs around here."

"Maybe so. But Mollie, take my word for it, Zach is important to the project. For more than one reason."

"Why?"

"I'm on the Eisenhower, Mollie, in the middle of rush hour. Just accept that I'm counting on you to pull in your horns and get along with Zach."

What was this? Aunt Gwen, who'd always urged Mollie to get with the right people and stay with the right people, was telling Mollie to cater to a streetwise semi-punk?

"You're not saying anything, Mollie. Does that mean you're sulking? Or you're thinking it over?"

Mollie pulled up her reserve patience. "I'm . . . thinking it over."

"Good. Hold on till this weekend, honey. I'll be down and we can have a long talk."

"I hope so!"

"I'm bringing that architect, Todd Wingate, to see what could be done to improve the exterior of the house." Aunt Gwen paused, as if searching her memory. "Let's see—didn't you meet Todd at my place a few weeks ago?"

"Uh—yes."

Mollie understood: Todd Wingate was another one of Aunt Gwen's little "accidents." An attractive, successful man who just happened to come by while Mollie was visiting her aunt.

"Anyway," Aunt Gwen continued, "that's the good news. The other news is that Sloan is also coming. I want her to see Indian Prairie."

Mollie had never met Sloan Harris. But she'd known for a long time that the relationship between Aunt Gwen and Henry Harris's twenty-year-old daughter by his first marriage was strained, to put it mildly. Sloan's mother had died young. According to Aunt Gwen, the first Mrs. Harris's East Coast family, so old and monied that "they think they invented New England," had pressured a grieving Henry Harris into turning Baby Sloan over to their cold care. She'd been brought up to look askance at "backwater" Illinois. And at her father, with his self-made business success. And certainly, at his second wife, with her strong will—and total disregard for their eminence.

After Mollie hung up the phone, she pondered for a moment. Aunt Gwen was executor of Uncle Henry's sizable estate, which was to be divided equally between her and Sloan. Except for Indian Prairie. That would be Sloan's alone at age twenty-one. But there was some sticking point about this, something Aunt Gwen had so far not discussed with Mollie.

Mollie admired Aunt Gwen's steadfast pursuit of personal goals. She loved Gwen's Michigan Avenue clothes and state-of-the-art makeup and North Shore mansion—all of which Gwen would gladly have shared with Mollie. But she and her aunt didn't always share the same perspective.

Take Aunt Gwen's reaction when Mollie suggested herself as the perfect person to set up Indian Prairie.

"It's not that I doubt your business ability," Aunt Gwen had argued. "You've got my knack for running things. But how can you leave your job in Chicago, with all its cultural advantages? Its excitement? Its . . . suitable men?"

"But I don't like city life. And I don't want to be one more faceless cog in a big company," Mollie had argued. "One day you're on your way up, the next you're downsized. Out."

Aunt Gwen had always preferred to make money the old-fashioned way: marry it. "That's where the suitable men come in, Mollie. Find one, and you can live in the country—on an estate. Not grubbing away on a farm." And then the final, desperate warning. "I'm so afraid you'll end up like your mother and dad. Poor."

Mollie hadn't irritated her aunt by mentioning that Mom and Dad were two of the happiest people she knew. Or that Aunt Gwen's plans for Mollie were usually a red flag to the bull in Jim Moreau.

"Kathy, what's your sister trying to do with Mollie, make a clone out of the kid?" Mollie's usually soft-spoken dad would growl.

"Why, Jim," Mom would intercede, "she loves Mollie like she was her own daughter—"

"Then why in the Sam Hill didn't she have her own daughter? She's sure been married enough times!"

Mollie knew the routine by heart. She couldn't help grinning now as she shook off her misgivings. She'd handle Indian Prairie Farm. Zach could sneer at Aunt Gwen, but Mollie wasn't sorry she'd inherited her aunt's iron resolve to do what she'd set out to do.

And the first thing Mollie had to do was swallow

her pride and make Zach's dinner. Something quick and easy. And loaded with arsenic?

Nah! He wasn't worth going to the state pen for.

Thirty minutes later, she placed a clean kitchen towel over a plate of savory soft-shell tacos and carried them and a can of cold soda outside to a picnic table standing under an apple tree.

''Zach?''

He came out of the toolshed carrying a tool chest.

''Dinner's ready,'' she said, looking just past his shoulder.

Zach set the chest back in the shed. ''Good thing Dad's coming down tomorrow with my tool supply,'' he remarked as he came toward her. ''There's not a lot here to work with.''

''You do this for a living?''

''For now, anyway.''

Mollie couldn't resist a jab. ''Really? Following Daddy into his business? Kind of . . . modeling yourself after a relative?''

He stopped short. He started to say something—a zinger, Mollie was sure—but changed his mind. ''If you don't mind, I'll wash up before I eat.''

He walked straight past her without waiting for a reply.

Mollie stewed about how to dismount from her high horse without falling on her face. With her two hungry farm cats, Sissy and Bro, prowling nearby she couldn't just walk off and leave the tacos sitting.

She picked up Sissy and began to pet her glossy tortoiseshell coat with short, impatient strokes. She glanced around at the large, disheveled house yard. It needed so much grooming. Last fall's leaves still moldered under towering oaks. Yet, with lots of flowering bushes and clumps of iris and peonies preparing to burst with May blooms, it promised an old-fashioned charm. And from the nearby woods seeped the earthy perfume of new timber grass fused with the sharp mint of pennyroyal.

Beyond the farmyard, some of the Indian Prairie hills were gentle enough for cultivation. But the middle portion of the land had been strip-mined for coal a half century ago, before government regulations forced coal companies to return mined-out land to its former state. So now, besides the original hills, deep mining trenches had created miniature mountains, covered with trees and brush, and several miles of small, clear lakes brimming with unpolluted fish. Old roads used by the coal trucks still wound through the property, perfect paths for riding and hiking.

Mollie's hand slowed on Sissy's fur. She gave the purring cat a soft kiss on the head and set her on the ground.

A deep breath of the fresh, cool air, and Mollie knew Uncle Henry was right about one thing. Indian Prairie was an ideal setting to take some sting out of harrassed spirits.

When Zach came back to the table, he'd taken off the baseball cap. His long hair was bound into a neat ponytail and his bronzed hands and clean nails smelled of soap.

He looped his tall frame onto the picnic bench, pulled the tab on the soda, and took a long swig. "Ahh! I needed that!"

Mollie started to walk away.

Zach stopped the soda can halfway to the tabletop. He gestured toward the covered plate of tacos. "Aren't you going to eat?"

"I'll . . . have something later," Mollie replied stiffly, her back to him. "In the house."

There was an instant's silence. Then a quiet, ironic, "Excuse me. Auntie Gwen didn't bring you up to eat with the hired help?"

Resentment flamed through Mollie. If there was one thing she wasn't, it was a snob. She pivoted toward Zach, intending to tell him off. But she was stopped by Aunt Gwen's admonition to get along with him. "It's not that," she said, forcing herself to sound reasonable. "I'm—just not hungry right now."

"Well, why not at least sit with me? We need to decide what needs fixing first if you're going to open this place within the next hundred years."

Reluctantly, Mollie came back to the picnic table and sat opposite Zach.

He lifted the cover on the tacos and sniffed. "Smells pretty good." A small imp teased in his dark eyes. He picked up a taco. "You make these from scratch?"

"Oh, yeah," Mollie said. "Even ground the corn for the soft shell, right out of the field."

"Sure you did," he joked. He bit into the taco and tasted critically. "Well, it's not genuine Mex, but you did all right." His eyes sparked again. "For a farm girl."

Mollie bit her tongue. "Look—I know you don't like me, but let's just aim for decency here, okay?"

"Good idea." He lifted the plate toward her. She noticed his hands; they looked strong and tough, but with a certain grace of line and proportion. Artisan hands. "Here. You better have one."

Mollie took one of the juicy tacos. It did taste good, but in a matter of seconds, she'd squirted filling onto her shirt.

Zach didn't comment, but she saw the tug of a suppressed grin as he ate with a neat dispatch that left him spotless.

"So," Zach began after they'd finished the brief meal. "What have you been doing, Mollie Moreau, since I used to rattle your cage?"

"Oh, the usual. College. A business degree. A couple of years working for Chicago Insurance."

"Yeah? And you gave all that up to come down here and run a vacation farm—that doesn't even exist?"

"Yet," Mollie corrected. "It will exist."

He took another swig of pop. "I've been wondering . . . I always liked Henry Harris; he was a straight shooter. But I didn't know he was into good works. At least, not so much that he'd sink a lot of dough into a project like this."

"Well, he grew up poor in the city, you know. He felt life had been good to him, so he wanted to give something back. A place where ordinary families without a lot of money could relax and enjoy. At least, that's what Aunt Gwen says motivated him."

"That sounds good. What's your motivation?"

"Why, I think Uncle Henry had a great idea. And this is exactly the kind of job I've always wanted."

He didn't say anything, just gazed at her with a half-smile—and some questions in his eyes.

Mollie hurried on, "As you've so nicely reminded me over the years, I *am* a farm girl. And I can't think of anything better than staying one. Plus, I've got a business degree. And after all Aunt Gwen's done for me, doesn't it seem natural I'd want to help her out now?"

"It seems natural you'd like running a business—your way."

Mollie's face heated. "I don't apologize for that."

The half-smile and the questions—neither went away. "Okay. Let me see if I've got this straight: Starting in June, you're going to house a few guests at a time in Old Ugly, here—" He pointed to the house. "And they're going to do what for fun, besides watch the grass grow? Milk the cows? Check the chickens?"

Mollie bottled her desire for a smart retort. "There won't be any cows or chickens. At least, for a while."

"Huh? I thought this was a farm."

"Without a varmint-proof pen, chickens are just coyote bait. And it's cheaper to buy milk at the store than feed and inoculate cows, then pasteurize the milk."

Zach reared back in mock alarm. "What's the world coming to? Farmers buying their milk and eggs at the local IGA? Scarfing down tacos instead of good old beefsteak and gravy?"

"Well, if you're really into barnyard life, I can introduce you to Ray Jones's beef cattle. You can even try to milk one—if you don't mind getting your head kicked off."

"You'd like that, wouldn't you?"

"Indian Prairie guests will go on trail rides, or long walks, or they'll fish or swim or boat in the strip mine lakes. Or maybe just wander out onto the prairie for some peace and quiet. Who knows, some of them might like to lie in a hammock and read a book."

"Wackos everywhere."

Mollie elected to ignore his baiting. "There's a place on the other side of the lakes—I call it the Outback—with some kind of . . . primitive facilities for tent campers."

Zach looked interested. "Yeah? How primitive?"

Mollie stirred uneasily. "Well, right now, just a lake, and . . . one of those rent-a-potties."

Zach laughed aloud. ''Primitive enough.''

''A farm is—'' Mollie paused. Zach would proba-bly hoot at her next statement. ''A farm can be a very good place. I—and my aunt—want Indian Prairie to do as much for the people who come here as Uncle Henry hoped it would.''

Zach didn't hoot. Instead, he regarded her thought-fully. ''And you're going to be in charge of every-thing? Except me?''

''I'll be in charge. Of everything.''

One of his straight eyebrows hooked.

Color rose in Mollie's face. ''You have a problem with a woman running things, don't you?''

Her restlessness increased under his strong, study-ing gaze.

''Well?'' she demanded.

''I don't have *any* problems with women just be-cause they're women.''

''Then what is it?''

His lips smiled, but his eyes didn't. ''You love your aunt, don't you? Look up to her?''

Mollie went immediately on the defensive. ''Of course I do! So?''

''If there's one thing I don't take, it's getting jerked around. So if you want me to do something, ask me straight out. Don't come at me with any sly stuff.''

''Sly stuff? What's that got to do with Aunt Gwen?''

He didn't answer, but his cool smile drove the im-plication home.

Hot with anger, Mollie lurched to her feet. Her flail-ing gesture of protest sent Zach's soda can spinning.

Chapter Three

"Where do you come off, attacking my Aunt Gwen?"

Zach slid back on the picnic bench to avoid the spurt of soda. "Who's attacking? I just want to know whether you plan to handle things the way she does—hold back facts and fudge the truth?"

Mollie's voice shook with wrath. "I don't think you can accuse *me* of holding back anything! I think I've always been plenty direct with *you!*"

Zach rose to get away from the soda puddling on the picnic bench. "That you have! But you've never been on your aunt's payroll before, have you?"

Mollie couldn't believe her ears. "You think I'd—? What has Aunt Gwen ever done to turn you against her—besides give you a *job*?"

There was a sudden tightening around Zach's eyes. "I've seen, and heard, a few things—" He stopped at Mollie's sharp frown. "But let's back off, get down to business. I need to inspect the house and see what kind of mess scared Dad."

Mollie was far more upset than she wanted him to know. Her breath was still coming hard as she led him into the house. But she forced her attention to the matters at hand. For sure, there were plenty of flaws in the old house for her to point out, besides the obvious ones. The upstairs bathtub drain that didn't work, the windows in the biggest bedroom that were stuck tight as a drum, the broken tread in the open staircase. She and Zach worked their way down to the basement, where, flashlight in hand, Zach examined floor joists and wiring and other drizzly but vital concerns.

"It's in a lot better shape than I'd have thought," he commented when they at last climbed the basement stairs. "The foundation is good, and the structure is built like iron." He glanced around the kitchen. "But it sure is grungy!"

"I won't argue that," Mollie agreed. "Uncle Henry left a fund for start-up expenses, but it'll only stretch so far. So Dee is going to help me spruce up the interior as best we can, as cheap as we can."

"What about all the other stuff that has to be done around here? The farming, and the nags?"

"Dee's husband, Raymond, will farm the crop land. And the horses are my responsibility."

"You like four-footed Harleys?"

"They're nicer than some people."

He took her point with a cool smile. "They take orders better, I'm sure." He plucked an apple from a bowl on the kitchen table and started munching. "I'm gonna ride my 'pony' back to that town I came through about ten minutes from here—Shawano, is it? See if they've got someplace cheap I can stay nights."

Oh-oh. Aunt Gwen had given Mollie express directions that Zach was to use the room Mollie had prepared for George Kincannon's stay. "I don't want you out there alone, Mollie," she'd said.

"I'd rather be alone than have Zach Kincannon underfoot twenty-four hours a day," Mollie had argued.

"Mollie—"

The tension in Aunt Gwen's voice had been real, a

reminder that she was going through a rough time. Mollie had said, ''Okay.''

''Aunt Gwen said for you to stay here. In the room I got ready for your dad.''

Zach's brows crinkled. ''I was pretty sure it wasn't your idea.''

Mollie ignored the gibe and crossed the living room to a door into the tacked-on annex. ''The sheets are clean, and you've got a bathroom,'' she said, pointing into a modest bedroom. ''It's as good as the motel in Shawano. And a lot better than a straw pile in the horse barn.''

Zach's smile was ironic. ''Well, who could resist a cordial invitation like that? And make Aunt Gwen mad?''

''Please—'' Mollie ground out. ''We've got our hands full here. Let's not bicker over a bedroom.''

He chuckled, slow and gruff. ''Okay I'll bring in my stuff. But I'm still going back into town for a while. See what's happening.'' He grinned at her frown. ''Want to come with me?''

''I prefer my head on my shoulders, not smashed into a highway.''

''You could wear my helmet.''

''No thanks.''

He shrugged. ''What time is breakfast?''

''Anytime you want to pour yourself a bowl of cornflakes,'' Mollie said coolly. ''I usually get up at five.''

''*Five?* In the *morning?*''

''No, the afternoon,'' Mollie replied sarcastically. ''Look, Zach, this job isn't going to be about *our* fun and games. It's about the animals' needs and the customers' good times. Maybe you ought to think it over.''

''If I had a choice, I would.'' Zach strolled to the door and out.

Within seconds, Mollie heard the Harley roar to life and spin down the lane toward the road.

That was a new one. It wasn't Zach Kincannon's idea to fill in for his father? Then why was he doing it? From what she'd seen of him, Mollie expected Zach to do what pleased Zach, not anybody else. Of course, what would an uneducated street bully do to make an honest living? Crochet doilies?

Mollie cleared up the kitchen, then checked to be sure the downstairs bathroom was supplied with towels and other essentials. It seemed unnaturally quiet.

Mollie had never been afraid to stay alone at home on the family farm fifty miles to the south. But then, it wasn't situated in the middle of nowhere. And the house wasn't big and rambling and full of still-unfamiliar corners.

Mollie turned on plenty of lights, got an apple in the kitchen, and went outside into the deepening twilight. She wandered down to the horse pasture and leaned against the wooden gate.

She whistled softly, and a small bay mare in the far corner pricked up her ears.

''Star! Come here, honey!'' Mollie coaxed the quarter horse Dad had bought her when she was fifteen.

Star came trotting. She stretched her sturdy neck across the gate to nuzzle the apple from Mollie's hand.

Mollie loved almost everything about horses—smell, whickering, warm hides, and distinct personalities. She was happy with the herd she'd bought from a going-out-of-business riding stable. Except for Star, the ponies were "grade" horses. Mixed breeds, a little on the old side—nice, reliable mounts for inexperienced riders. Tony, Whip, Babe, Sally, Ginger, Suzi, Robb Roy, Silky, Jurvis, Pet, and Romeo: They'd come as a smooth-riding package. Almost. Then there was Junior.

Junior was a young gelding, barely trained. He was supposed to be mostly Appaloosa, but Mollie was sure that somewhere under his spotted brown-and-white hide ran the blood of a Clydesdale. Junior was huge! He stood nearly sixteen hands at the shoulder; he bulged with muscles where an Appie should be slim.

And he had a mind of his own. A goofy one, to Mollie's thinking. But if she could train him properly, Junior would be a good mount for the occasional big-guy rider, the three-hundred-pounder who'd squash a regular pony to the ground. Plus, the more she'd observed the horse, the more she'd been convinced that his life with a less than understanding master was going to be rough. If she didn't take him . . .

She'd taken him. So now Junior was trying to butt in on Mollie and Star. He pushed up beside the little bay mare, but Star hadn't gotten her name from the small white splash on her forehead. No, she was star temperament. She shared Mollie's attentions with nobody. Her ears went back.

"Take a hint, Junior!" Mollie warned.

Too late. Lightning fast, Star wheeled and delivered a resounding kick toward the gelding's mottled hindquarters. Junior reared back just in time to escape serious injury. He snorted and pawed the ground and regarded Star with a fierce eye, then turned and ambled away with an insolent sway to his big rump.

"Good idea, Junior," Mollie murmured through a

grin. She gave Star a final ear scratch and went back into the house and up to her room on the second floor. While she slipped on her oversized sleep T-shirt, she couldn't help listening for the return of the Harley. She got into bed, and turned on her mini TV for the ten o'clock news.

Murder, theft, political chicanery—the usual stuff. She channel surfed. What did she want to go to sleep on? A talk show host slavering over a big blond in a small dress? A muscle bound movie hero terminating New York City? A sitcom family playing to canned laughter? She snapped off the tube and turned out the light.

Her ears seemed to pick up everything. Off in the distance an eerie yip-yipping shrilled. She knew it was just coyotes after some unlucky deer or rabbit. Still, the hair stirred on the back of her neck.

She wondered what Zach was up to in town. Probably hanging out at a bar. Maybe flirting with that waitress at the Farmer's Inn. She seemed like the type ready to flip over an outlaw. . . .

Underneath Mollie's thoughts ran a statement. *''I've seen—and heard—some things . . .''*

What could Zach have seen or heard to make him so turned-off her aunt? True, Aunt Gwen used to come down pretty hard on the juvenile Zach when she caught him picking on Mollie. But hadn't he asked for it?

It wasn't until she finally heard the motorcycle rumble up the drive, and Zach enter through the kitchen door, that Mollie was able to turn over and drift off. . . .

Scra-a-a-tch . . .
Mollie opened one eye, dragged from early sleep.

Thu-u-mp . . . th-u-u-d . . .

Mollie came to full consciousness. Her bedroom was directly above the long front porch. Something was down there, something stealthy. More soft thuds and crunches—was someone trying to break into the house?

Mollie froze for a second, then, trembling, slid out of bed and into her jeans and shoes. She crept down the stairs, ears straining. Something brushed against the front door; then the knob began to rattle. Fear leaped in her throat. She forced herself down the last step, intending to peek out a window beside the door.

''Unh-h-h!''

Mollie's gasp was stifled by a firm, warm hand pressed across her lips.

''Shh.''

She felt herself pulled against a big masculine frame; she nearly tore her head off twisting to see Zach's face inches from hers.

''Wait here,'' Zach whispered. ''I'm going to sneak out the back door and see what's up.''

Mollie couldn't have answered if she'd wanted to.

Zach slipped out of the room. The doorknob rattled once again, and Mollie's heart rocketed against her ribs.

For a second there was dead silence, then a yell from Zach, followed by a terrific stomping and clattering.

''Zach!'' She raced to the front door and unlocked it with trembling fingers. ''Zach!'' She threw the door open. ''Are you all right?''

''I don't know! When was the last time this thing ate?''

Mollie rushed out. A few feet off the porch, almost

head-to-head with Zach, stood a huge, white, four-footed figure.

Molly let out a long, relieved breath. ''Junior!'' she yelped. ''How did you get out?''

'' 'Junior?' '' Zach repeated incredulouly. ''If this is Junior, I'd hate to see Senior!''

''Junior, you idiot,'' Mollie scolded, ''what are you doing on the front porch?''

Junior's answer was a contemptuous snort that said it all: ''I go where I want.''

''And what's that hanging out of your mouth?'' Mollie moved closer to the horse. ''Good night! You've got that old cornhusk wreath somebody left on the front doorknob!''

''So I'm not the only one who has to find his own grub,'' Zach remarked.

''What do you want to do, choke on a staple?'' Mollie inquired. She ended a short tug-of-war by wrenching the tattered wreath free from Junior's mouth. ''If you're out, I suppose the rest of the herd is, too.''

She stepped off the porch and headed for the pasture gate. Zach came with her.

Sure enough, the gate was open. It was moonlight; dark forms could be seen roaming down the lane, headed for the main road.

''How'd this happen?'' Zach inquired, examining the opened gate latch.

''I'm not sure,'' Mollie said, ''but it happened last week, too, right after I brought in the last of the herd. Which was Junior.''

She felt a large, soft nose rubbing on her shoulder. She turned around to face the troublemaking horse. ''Don't try to make up, kiddo. You've been bad.''

"And you wonder why I like Harleys?" Zach scoffed.

Mollie drove Junior into the pasture, then whistled to lure the rest of the herd back. Fat chance! They were off on an adventure. Even Star played deaf.

"Zach, would you keep an eye on the gate so Junior doesn't get out again?" Mollie requested. "But stay out of sight when I get the other horses headed this way."

She jumped into the pickup and maneuvered carefully down the lane after the wanderers. Sweat broke out on her forehead as she saw car lights approaching on the main road. If the horses spooked . . .

The pickup glided along the shoulder past one horse after another. In the nick of time, Mollie got ahead of the herd, sped up, and parked sideways across the end of the lane. A vehicle whizzed past on the main road, then she could let out her breath. Five minutes more, and she had the herd trotting through the pasture gate.

Zach appeared with a strand of heavy wire, which he wound between the top of the gate and the adjoining fence. "That'll hold 'em in the rest of the night—unless Junior's packing wire clippers. I'll figure out something better in the morning."

Zach was clad only in jeans and moccasins. Mollie watched the play of midnight moon over his broad, bare shoulders and powerful back as he gave the wire one last twist. He turned toward her. A sense, a realization that Zachary Kincannon's attractions were undeniable—and far more than physical—shook Mollie.

"I—uhh—" She wanted to say a simple "Thank you," but the words stuck. "I . . . owe you. For coming to my rescue," she added lamely.

Zach didn't say anything, but he was close enough

that she could feel the warmth coming off his body. He didn't smell of liquor. Or cheap cologne. Just clean, healthy man-skin.

"I mean—" Mollie rubbed her forearm nervously. "It could have been somebody dangerous on the porch. Not just an overgrown pony."

"Yeah. That's right," Zach said quietly.

The following instant of silence seemed about two miles long. "Everybody's been telling me I'm not safe out here nights," Mollie said, flustered. "I . . . guess they can stop worrying, can't they? I mean, with you here?"

Zach's hands rested on his hips. She could feel, rather than see, his eyes holding hers. "That's supposed to be a compliment?"

"Well—you know what I mean," Mollie stammered.

"No. Tell me."

Mollie studied him. He was young and powerful, agile as a cat. He could subdue her in a breath if he wanted to. But he'd used that all-out masculinity to protect her. Something very strong, very exciting, began to rill around her heart.

"I mean—" she stumbled, "I don't think you'd . . . hurt me."

He frowned, but a sly grin tugged at his lower lip. "Yeah? What happened to 'street boy'? 'Jerk'? Oh, and did I miss any other nice names?"

"I just mean—you may be a pain in the neck sometimes, but you're not a slimeball."

"Hey!" He shook his head, a low chuckle underlying his response. "Baby, you've sure got a way with words. You don't know how good that makes me feel."

"You shouldn't call me 'baby.' "

"That's a bad word?" he quizzed.

"It's . . . cheap, sleazy."

"You've been running with the wrong crowd. When I say 'baby,' I can mean anything from 'young lady' to 'sweet armful.' You got a better substitute?"

Mollie's shoulders raised. She couldn't resist a smile. "Okay. You stuck your neck out for me tonight, so I guess that entitles you to a liberty or two."

"Good. 'Cause I want to exercise one right now."

Mollie stepped back. "Huh?"

"I'm starved, Mollie. 'Please, Mr. Bumble—may I have some more porridge?' "

Mollie laughed aloud at the piping Oliver Twist voice. "After the scare I've had, the kitchen—the entire food supply—is at your disposal."

They started back across the farmyard. Mollie felt a need to do something, any small thing, to show Zach she was less hostile. "Come to think of it," she said, speeding up to match his long stride, "I'm kind of hungry, too. Want to share a snack?"

Zach's "Sure," was soft; they walked on, close, but not touching.

Chapter Four

Five in the morning, and Mollie was already out in the horse barn filling feedboxes. In spite of a scant four hours' sleep, she felt great! She'd actually set a breakfast table for Zach, with frozen waffles waiting in the toaster, and several strips of bacon ready for the microwave. She told herself it was just the decent thing to do after last night.

He liked food, that was for sure. Turned loose with the groceries last night, he'd concocted a monster sandwich out of French bread, pizza sauce, leftover taco meat, cheese, and just about anything else that couldn't run away. Then he'd made her try it, and she'd had to admit it was good.

She smiled now, remembering the fits and starts of their conversation at the midnight table. It was hard for either to approach the other without sniping, but they'd made an effort. Zach could be witty, really humorous, and mostly at his own expense.

One subject, however, did not strike him funny.

Mollie had finally come right out and asked him why he was at Indian Prairie if he didn't want to be. His reply was slow in coming, and guarded.

''Let's just say I need to pay off a debt to your aunt. And she thinks this is the way for me to pay it.''

''But why . . . ?''

He'd laughed then, but his eyes had turned very

black. "You know Gwen. She's always got an agenda."

Mollie had started to defend her aunt, but what he said was true. She'd let the matter drop.

Mollie filled a small bucket with oats and plucked a halter from the wall. Every trail herd needed a lead horse to lure the others in from the pasture as well as to head the trail ride columns. Was there any question as to who that should be?

In the pasture, Star grazed alone near the pond. Mollie approached her, proffering the bucket and keeping the halter out of sight. Once her nose discovered the oats, Star let Mollie slip the halter over her head and lead her into the barn. A few coaxing whistles, and the other horses followed.

In the barn, all the horses managed to find their rightful stalls, except for—who else?—Junior. He tried to bully his way into several different spots before kicks, bites, and a lot of indignant squeals forced him to accept his place at the end of the line.

Once the horses were tied to the rings above their feedboxes, Mollie began the rest of the daily routine, brushing sleek hides, checking legs for any injuries or swellings, picking out small rocks from the hooves.

By six-thirty, Star and two other horses were saddled for a morning practice ride. Before any paying customers climbed aboard one of her ponies, Mollie had to know the herd was comfortable with the new terrain as well as with the new leader, Star.

A car drove in; Mollie assumed it was Dee getting an early start on the kitchen scrub-down. Mollie turned the "off-duty" steeds into the pasture. Junior bolted out ahead of the others.

"He's a rude one."

The deep male voice whirled Mollie toward the open barn door. ''Oh!''

''Didn't mean to scare you.'' It was Todd Wingate, all six golden feet of him, framed in the doorway, sun rays glancing off his shiny blond curls. Ahh! Was he good looking!

''Todd.'' Mollie went toward him, hand outstretched. ''Aunt Gwen said you'd be down this weekend. This is only Thursday.''

''I had an appointment in the Quad Cities yesterday,'' he said, mentioning a four-city enclave clustered on both sides of the Mississippi, some forty miles to the west. His even grin lit up dark green eyes. ''So I thought, 'Why go back to Chicago when I can spend an extra day in the country with a beautiful girl?' ''

Mollie laughed. She knew an old smoothie when she met one. ''Would you like some coffee?'' she asked.

''Thought you'd never ask!''

The two started across the farmyard toward the house.

''Why are you up so early in the morning?'' Todd wanted to know.

Mollie jerked her thoughts away from the neat fit of his faded jeans and sage corduroy jacket. She'd bet he paid a lot for the studied casual look of his clothes and hair. ''I'm just about to take some horses out on a practice run. I don't suppose you ride?''

''Do I ride?'' Todd turned back to Mollie, and she caught a faint drift of pricey aftershave. ''You name it, I can ride it! And what's more—'' He took off his jacket and slung it through the open window of his black GMC Jimmy. ''I'd like to give that big horse— the feisty one—a lesson in manners before long.''

"Junior? You'd better eat your Wheaties before you take him on," Mollie remarked.

"Better yet, bacon and eggs."

While they walked toward the house, Todd told Mollie about growing up on a big estate in northern Illinois. "My dad was the manager. I learned early how to take care of the owner's Arabians. Did such a good job, Mr. Murton bought me a cow pony as a reward. The rest is history."

Todd's own grin took the offense out of his breezy bragging.

The two stopped where they could get a full view of the house. "Think you might have your work cut out for you?" Mollie queried as Todd studied the homely structure, a bemused expression on his clean-featured face.

He shook his head. "It looks like it started out about the turn of the century as an honest I-house. You know, two stories, two rooms wide and one room deep. The flaring eaves and little casement windows on the back addition? Somebody's idea of Dutch colonial."

"And what do you call the addition on this side, with the flat roof and yellow siding? And the gorgeous green roof over the porch?"

"Sick."

Mollie laughed. " 'Is there hope for this marriage?' "

Todd put a comradely hand on Mollie's shoulder. "The difficult takes me a while, the impossible just a little longer."

Mollie led Todd around to the kitchen door. He stopped at sight of the old Harley lolling near the picnic table. "Whoa! What have we got there?"

"A grown man's play-toy?"

Todd walked closer, inspecting the Harley with interest. "A grown man's fantasy. A Harley-Davidson Duo-Glide. 'They don't hardly make 'em that way no more.' "

"That's bad?"

Todd grinned. "That's good—if you own one. A panhead FL, hardtail—this ol' hog was made in the days when men were still men and didn't get bashed for it! Somebody's got some money. It's worth real dough."

"You're kidding! It looks pretty beat up to me."

"It wasn't bought to look pretty in the driveway. Duos were made for a short time in the late fifties; extremely rare. With a little spit and polish . . . Man! I'd take it in a minute!"

Zach came out the kitchen door, pulling a headband over his forehead. He and Todd regarded each other with surprise.

"Zach, Aunt Gwen's architect is here. Zach Kincannon, Todd Wingate."

Todd offered his hand. " 'Kincannon,' as in 'son of George Kincannon, all-purpose repairman?' "

"That's right." Zach gave him a firm handshake.

"Your dad does good work. In fact, I expected him to carry out a lot of the changes I'll make here."

Zach laughed. "Dad's gotten smarter as he got older. So—I'm here; he's in Chicago."

Todd nodded toward the Harley. "I've just been admiring your bike. Had it long?"

"Nope."

Todd walked around the cycle. "Makes me wonder if I'm in the wrong business. If I ever rob a bank, I'll give you a good price for it."

Zach smiled, but his already dark eyes turned opaque. "If I ever have a good reason to sell it, I'll give you first chance." He came down off the last step, close to Mollie. "I'm going to fix the pasture gate right now. I don't mind losing sleep over a good-lookin' girl, but—" He gestured toward Junior watching them from the horse pasture. "Not at the whim of that overgrown oat-burner."

He sauntered a few steps toward the toolshed, then turned back. "By the way, Mollie, thanks for the breakfast. You're gonna spoil me."

Heat came up in Mollie's face. Why was Zach hinting there was more than ... business in their relationship?

Todd didn't say anything for a second, then shrugged and turned to Mollie. "Didn't you promise me some food?"

"Oh—yes."

Zach was watching her with a half-grin. Was she going to tell the handsome architect to get his own cornflakes?

"I'll fix you some waffles," Mollie said, heading into the house. "The same as Zach had."

Todd followed her. "Sounds like I may have come late to the party."

Mollie snorted. "There is nothing—and I mean *nothing*—between Zach and me but business. And some past bad vibes."

Todd took a seat at the kitchen table. "Really? I'd say Biker Pal's planning to add some sweet spice to those vibes in the near future."

The deep woods of the Outback were silent except for the squeak of leather and the throp-throp of horses' hooves on the dusty path worn by generations of cattle. Mollie rode Star, holding a lead rope to Tony, who in turn led Ginger tethered to his saddle horn. On the fourth horse, Whip, sat Todd, leading Romeo and Robb Roy in similar fashion. The caravan pulled up under a magnificent oak tree on the edge of a clearing. Mollie prepared to dismount.

Todd slid off Whip like the riding pro he'd proved to be and caught her lightly around the waist as she swung off Star's back. His hands were very firm, very sure.

Mollie spoke carefully. "Thank you." She moved to lead Star and her other two ponies to the small stream gurgling a few feet away.

Todd did likewise with his horses. After the ponies had drunk their fill, they grazed, reins dropped in ground ties, while Todd took Mollie by the hand to a soft mound of new timber grass.

They were at the highest point of the Indian Prairie property, atop a long hill framed on either side by heavy timber. Below them, miles of rolling prairie spilled to the horizon. Todd sat, and pulled Mollie down beside him.

"I always knew Henry Harris had an eye for good property," Todd said, "and this view proves it."

"It is beautiful, isn't it?" Mollie agreed. "There's not much land like this left in northern Illinois. Uncle Henry was lucky to find it for his project."

Todd's generous lips pulled at one corner. "Ah, yes—his project. Providing rest and recreation for the financially challenged. That's going to pay out?"

"Well, if we're careful—and lucky—we'll be okay."

Todd regarded her with a doubting smile. " 'Okay?'

Don't you know this property, with smart development, could be worth millions?''

''Indian Prairie isn't about money, Todd. It's . . . about carrying out Uncle Henry's dream. He wanted to do something good for ordinary people.''

Todd's smile stayed. But his eyes were serious. ''Honey, just about everything comes down to money. And as far as 'ordinary' goes—'' He shook his head. ''I don't have much time for it.''

Mollie shifted, a little annoyed.

''I think you could use some financial advice,'' Todd said. His grin turned one-sided. ''I mean, Easy Rider's got great muscles, but what does he know about business?''

Mollie had been mighty glad to have Zach's great muscles flex between her and possible danger last night. She answered with some coolness, ''I don't know—or care—what Zach knows about business. I need a repairman, not a mentor.''

Todd grinned, casually chewing a sprig of blue grass. ''I read you. I like a filly with spirit. But don't get too sharp with me. Who knows, someday I may be able to help you out.''

Don't hold your breath, Mollie thought.

Blu-u-r-p, bl-blur-r-p, bl-u-r-p!

A motorcycle was belching its way over the woods path.

Todd frowned. ''Some people haven't heard—three's a crowd.''

Within seconds, Zach roared up on the old Harley and bounced to a stop.

Mollie leaped to her feet and caught Whip's reins as he jerked away from the untoward noise. The other steeds danced in place, nervous.

"Zach, keep that thing away from the horses!" Mollie warned. "They hate loud noises."

Zach shut down the motor. "This bike purrs like a kitten."

"More like a sick tomcat!"

Zach grinned and gestured toward the nervous horses. "At least it doesn't take a Harley and two spares to get me where I'm going."

"These aren't spares." Mollie explained the reason for the extra horses.

Zach dismounted the Harley and flopped down on the ground where Mollie had been sitting. He gazed out toward the horizon. "I have to admit, there's a lot to please the eye out here. Wouldn't you say, Wingate?"

Todd rose with his usual easy grace. He took Whip's reins from Mollie, smiling into her eyes. "There sure is. Let's go, Mollie."

Zach's grin hardened slightly. But he kept his eyes on the horizon. "Wait a minute. I can see where the 'prairie' comes from in 'Indian Prairie.' But what about the 'Indian'? Where does that come in?"

Mollie wasn't altogether irked by Zach's noisy intrusion. Todd was beginning to wear on her. "Because," she said, "there used to be many tribes here. Thousands of years ago, this area was one of the richest hunting grounds in central North America. Later, a bison trail became the Great Sauk Trail. It actually cut across the corner of the Outback."

"Do tell! Where was everybody going?"

"The Sauk and Fox, among other tribes, made regular trips—business trips—between what's now Rock Island and Detroit."

Zach's brows hiked. "Business trips? You're puttin' me on! Braves with briefcases?"

Twenty-four hours ago, Mollie would have fired over his teasing. Now she just grinned. "No, street boy. With trade goods. They bought and sold from the British and the French. That is, when they weren't making war on one faction or the other."

"Treacherous devils!"

Mollie shook her head violently. "That's not true. At least they didn't treat the white man any worse than he treated them."

"You sound like a sympathizer."

"Well, sheesh! You'd have to be blind not to see the Indians got a bum deal! The Blackhawk War, which pretty much ended Indian occupation of Illinois—even white people living through it said it was wrong."

Zach's gaze, the crooked smile quirking his lips, stopped Mollie's heated protest.

"You know a lot about these dudes, do you?" he queried softly.

"No." Mollie smiled again. There was no sarcasm in Zach's teasing. "But the county historical society does. I did my homework. Otherwise, how can I answer Indian Prairie guests' curiosity about its history?"

Zach's smile lingered. "How, indeed?"

Mollie turned away, checking Tony's lead rope to escape Zach's taunting eyes.

As for Zach, he yawned lazily and stretched his long, sinewy body. "Wonder how many tired Big Chiefs have sacked out right here after a hard day on the trail?" He lay back, his arms beneath his head, and closed his eyes. "I know it sure suits me."

"Feel free to stay as long as you want," Todd put in wryly.

Mollie chuffed. "Zach, aren't you supposed to be working on the plumbing or something?"

"I'm waiting for Dad to get here with some special tools," Zach murmured. "Besides, I need a break. I didn't get much sleep last night. Remember?"

Mollie flushed. Todd stepped toward her and put a possessive arm around her shoulder. "I'm getting hungry, Mollie. Let's go back and I'll take you into town for lunch."

"Oh, fine," she agreed. This guy-thing between Zach and Todd—two grown men, both attractive, both probably at no loss for female admirers—they just had to one-up each other in front of her? Not that she minded starring in their attentions . . .

She walked over and nudged Zach's side with the toe of her boot. "Big Chief, I suggest you cut your siesta short. Aunt Gwen and her stepdaughter aren't going to like it tomorrow if they have to take a bath in the horse pond."

Zach sat up slowly, a wry grin on his face. "You 'suggest,' ma'am? Usually you order. You're gettin' real polite, ma'am!"

Mollie slapped a rein over Star's neck. "Zach, you call me 'ma'am' once more, I'm gonna run Star right over you!" She and Todd mounted and started to lead the extra horses back onto the path.

"Oh, by the way—"

Mollie wheeled Star to hear what Zach had to say.

He rose and ambled over to take hold of Star's bridle. Mollie's eyes got caught in his long, full gaze. Something startling, something—sweet and spicy—flickered there.

"Well?" she finally demanded. Why was her breath coming a bit fast?

Zach's face was sober, but his eyes . . . their black depths were dancing again.

"The Indians—are there any around here now?"

"Okay," Mollie said with an impatient grin, "you've had your fun at my expense. The plumbing?" She jerked a thumb in the direction of the house. "You want to take care of it—*please?*"

"If I have to."

"Good!" Mollie wheeled Star toward the house.

"Wait—"

She turned back. "Yes?"

His eyes were so warm and dark, so shining with fun. And undisguised attraction. Warmth, like a soft wind, flowed through Mollie. Suddenly she was back in the darkened house, his arms were pulling her close—and safe—from whatever was threatening from the porch. . . .

Zach's voice was soft and teasing. "I heard somewhere that Indians had a real thing for red hair. You sure some holdout Hiawatha isn't lurking in the bushes, just waiting to carry you off?"

Mollie's slow grin matched the sparkle in his eyes. "Chill, baby," she murmured. The blood beat against her throat. "My scalp is safe. But I can't guarantee your hind end if you don't get that plumbing fixed!"

She swung Star and nudged her into a fast trot.

Chapter Five

The convertible, a bright yellow Saab, cruised into the Indian Prairie drive. On the front porch, Mollie did a fast mental check: Bedrooms cleaned? Yep. Food prepared? Yep. Plumbing in order? Yep—thanks to Zach, who'd worked on it till four this morning. Business matters lined up for Aunt Gwen's perusal? Yep and double yep.

The Saab came to a gravel-spitting halt in the farmyard. *Neat car,* Mollie decided. *Somebody's been kind.*

Aunt Gwen got out on the passenger's side, pulling a silk scarf off her expensively blonded hair. Diamond rings glinted as she straightened the jacket of her natural linen pants suit.

''Aunt Gwen!'' Mollie came down off the porch to hug her beloved aunt. As usual, a delightful perfume wafted around Gwen Harris's well-toned person.

''Mollie.'' Aunt Gwen smiled and pulled back to look at her niece. Mollie was jarred by the tension around her aunt's clear blue eyes.

Aunt Gwen turned toward the Saab. ''Mollie, I'd like you to meet Henry's daughter, Sloan. Sloan, my niece and business associate, Mollie Moreau.''

From the driver's side of the Saab, Sloan Harris emerged. She was tall and slender in white shorts and a pink silk shirt opening over a matching halter. She moved toward Mollie with laid-back grace.

"How do you do, Sloan?"

Sloan offered a narrow, creamy-tan hand. Mollie couldn't see her eyes behind her dark glasses, but she had a feeling Sloan's cool smile didn't extend that far.

"I've heard about you," Sloan said in a low, lazy husk. Her handshake was firm but fleeting.

"Ah—yes, I'm sure," Mollie said after a second. "Shall we go into the house? Lunch is ready."

Mollie and her aunt chatted about small matters as the three turned toward the house. After two steps, Sloan stopped cold. Slowly she raised the dark glasses to rest on the short, straight dark hair swinging over her left eye in a clever asymetrical cut.

"*This* is the . . . house?"

Aunt Gwen cleared her throat. "Well, obviously, it needs some work—"

"Ha!"

Already, Mollie was ticked.

The trio proceeded into the house. Mollie watched Sloan's small, shapely figure move beneath her short-shorts. *To kill for,* Mollie groaned inwardly.

Four of the other lunchers were already standing by their places at the round oak dining table. Mollie introduced Todd, Ray, and Dee with a brief explanation as to where each fit into the Indian Prairie picture.

Aunt Gwen was gracious, of course. But Sloan? She barely glanced at the others; her eyes were roving the dingy walls and sparse, outdated furniture.

Dee brought in the family-style meal: lasagna, dill bread, mixed green salad, all freshly made. Her full, pretty face glowed with pride in her first real meal for Indian Prairie Farm.

"Shall we wait for Zach?" Mollie suggested. "He's seeing his dad off to Chicago."

''My,'' Aunt Gwen said, as the aroma from the lasagna wafted her way, ''this does smell wonderful!''

Ray Jones, big, sunburned, jovial, beamed. ''Dee's a great cook!''

''And, I hear, a very knowledgeable one,'' Aunt Gwen remarked. ''Mollie tells me Dee is a registered dietician.''

Sloan's brow raised. ''And she's working at Indian Prairie?''

Dee was just slipping into her place beside Ray. Her fair-skinned face turned a bright pink. ''The places that usually hire dieticians,'' she said carefully, ''hospitals and schools, are forty miles from here. I'd rather spend that driving time with my husband.''

Sloan's reply was a slight smirk.

''I consider us extremely lucky to have Dee,'' Mollie said, stiff with controlled irritation.

''And so will you, Sloan, once you've tasted this lunch!'' Ray promised.

Zach came into the dining room, heading off whatever further annoyance Sloan was planning to utter. He smiled at Mollie as he took a seat opposite her. ''Sorry I'm late,'' was his brief apology.

Mollie smiled back, relieved to finally get this meal off the ground. ''Sloan, I'd like you to meet Zachary Kincannon.''

Sloan's gaze flicked from the napkin she'd been unfolding with bored indifference—and stayed a long second on Zach's face. A smile, ever so slight, played at her lips. ''Oh, yes,'' she murmured softly. ''Gwen has mentioned your name.''

Zach uttered a dry cough. ''I'll bet she has.''

Mollie jumped into the breach. ''Well, let's not let this lovely food get cold.''

Within minutes, everyone's attention focused on Dee's superb culinary skills.

Everyone's but Sloan's, that is. Her smile was less than enthusiastic as she picked at her tiny serving of lasagna. She ate no bread, and, of course, turned down the dessert, apple crunch à la mode. Only salad, uncontaminated by dressing, passed her lusciously full lips. She looked often at Zach. Often.

Against her will, Mollie began to assess Sloan's effect on the three young males at the table. Ray, deep in love with his new bride, seemed totally unaware that Sloan found him boring. Todd made sure she knew who he was, what he did, and how well he did it.

But it was Zach's reaction that gave Mollie a little jolt around the heart. He listened to Aunt Gwen's light chatter, he laughed at Ray's jokes, but his eyes dwelt on Sloan.

Zach, do you really think you've got a chance with that lady? Mollie wondered. *I can tell what she thinks of Ray, Dee, and me—hicks. Todd's overconfidence leaves her cold. And you, Zach? Probably considers you just one more Chicago hood.*

Yet when Zach excused himself early to get back to the rewiring he was doing in an upstairs bedroom, Sloan rose quickly.

''Zach?''

He turned at her low-pitched command.

''Would you mind carrying up some heavy bags from the car?''

Mollie's hand tightened around her water glass. What did Sloan think Zach was, a bellhop?

Sloan brushed her forelock behind her ear. She

smiled. ''Gwen brought all the things that make her beautiful.''

If Aunt Gwen's smile had been a gun, Sloan would have dropped dead.

''Well—sure.'' Zach smiled back at Sloan.

Mollie sizzled. She couldn't hear the rest of the lunch-hour conversation; her ears were glued to the distinctive husk of Sloan's voice intermingled with Zach's deep tones as they brought in bags and ascended the hall staircase. Sloan didn't return to the lunch table.

''Well, uh—'' Dee mumbled into the uncomfortable quiet, ''I've got a full afternoon ahead. Want to help me clear, sweetie?''

''Love to,'' Ray affirmed, following her to the kitchen with hands full of dishes. Mollie glimpsed them sharing a soul-satisfying kiss just through the door.

''Mollie,'' Aunt Gwen murmured with a wry smile, ''maybe this would be a good time for our talk?''

''The sooner, the better.''

Mollie led her aunt into what had once been the living room but was now designated the ''guests' lounge.'' So far it sported one piece of furniture, a worn brown leather couch Mollie had picked up in a Shawano secondhand store.

She and Aunt Gwen took seats and Mollie dispensed with preliminaries. ''You said you'd explain to me why it was so important for me to be nice to Zach.''

''That's still hard to do?''

Mollie didn't answer Aunt Gwen's half-teasing probe.

"I thought I caught something . . . a little friendly between you two when Zach sat down to the table?"

Mollie avoided her aunt's eyes. Aunt Gwen could be very astute when it came to male-female relationships. "I was glad for anything that would break in on Sloan's sniping."

"Oh. I assumed you'd noticed—Zach's grown into a very attractive young man."

"He's . . . tolerable," Mollie said shortly. "But why is that important?"

Her aunt sat back, rubbing her temples, careful not to disturb her makeup. "Well, that's a story. You know the terms of Henry's will—Indian Prairie is in trust for Sloan, with me as trustee, until she reaches twenty-one this October."

"Yes. And now that I've met Sloan, well, I can't quite figure out why Uncle Henry left Indian Prairie to her. I mean, Sloan fits this place like a hand in a shoe."

Aunt Gwen shut her eyes tiredly. "I see that. You see that. But her father didn't." Aunt Gwen opened her eyes. "Henry was a good husband, the best I've had yet. Responsible, caring. That's why after he got over the shock of his first wife's death, he felt tremendous guilt that he'd let his daughter go to her grandparents. She was so obviously growing up spoiled and restless." Aunt Gwen rose and straightened a window shade. She shook her head wonderingly. "It always amazed me—a man as business-smart as Henry, so clueless when it came to his daughter."

Mollie frowned in puzzlement.

"No matter what Henry did," Aunt Gwen continued, "like buying Sloan that convertible for her twentieth birthday, it was never enough to win her affection. Or her attention.''

''It would have won mine!''

''Of course it would, Mollie. Because you and I and Henry grew up poor; we appreciate fine gifts when they come our way. But the East Coast Sloans are very much wrapped up in their own high-society lives. So they've thrown money at their granddaughter all her life. It wasn't until a few months before his death that Henry realized nothing he could buy would ever move Sloan out of her self-centered ways. Except one purchase—Indian Prairie.''

''How so?''

''Henry became convinced that if he could just get Sloan out here into the heart of the Midwest, get her involved in his dream for Indian Prairie Farm, she might develop some interests, some values, beyond the end of her nose.''

Mollie looked skeptical.

''My reaction exactly,'' Aunt Gwen agreed. ''But it was Henry's property, and Henry's daughter. I wasn't going to add to the anguish of his last days by telling him I thought the plan was impossible.''

Mollie sat forward. ''All right. But where does Zach fit in?''

Aunt Gwen's gaze strayed. ''There's a little bit more to Henry's last wishes than what went down on the will.''

''Yes?'' Why was Aunt Gwen looking so uneasy?

''Henry wanted to make sure Sloan married somebody strong enough—man enough, if you will—to deal with her self-absorption. Not to mention her sizable fortune. He had a secret candidate in mind.''

Mollie emitted a dry chuckle. ''Who? Superman?''

"Much closer to home. Zach."

The name hit Mollie like a bolt of lightning. She stared at her aunt, incredulous. "Penniless, streetwise, Harley-riding Zachary Kincannon?"

Aunt Gwen waved off Mollie's objection. "One mistake Henry never made—nor do I, for that matter— was to judge a person's character by his pocketbook."

"Aunt Gwen, how many times have you told me any man seems taller, handsomer, more desirable when he stands on a pile of money?"

Aunt Gwen smiled. "I firmly believe it. But it doesn't make him bad or good. Anyway, Sloan doesn't need a man with money. She'll inherit even more from her grandparents than she will from Henry. Besides, I don't think Zach needs much help in the taller, hand-somer, more desirable departments. Do you?"

Mollie chose to bypass that question. "Do you think spending money on that dumb motorcycle shows Zach's good business sense?"

Aunt Gwen made a pooh-poohing gesture. "That Harley is some old thing Henry took years ago in a real estate deal with a down-and-out actor—no, *not* Elvis!" she added with a slight laugh. "I sold it to Zach for a couple of hundred dollars after he found it moldering in a storage unit."

"But—" Mollie stopped, deciding this wasn't the time to tell her aunt what Todd had said about the bike. "That still leaves 'penniless' and 'streetwise.' "

"Ha! You haven't paid any repairmen lately, have you? The good ones—and that includes the Kincan-nons—pull down a pretty penny! And as to Zach's education, he's got a mixture of college and some very high-tech military training."

''Wait a minute! Wait a minute!'' Mollie drew in a troubled breath. ''Zach was in the service?''

''Oh, yes. College was too tame for him. So after a couple of years, he enlisted in the Marines. Got into some sort of 'special forces.' I imagine getting shot at on a few far-off 'peace missions' provided plenty of excitement!''

Mollie frowned. ''I'm confused.''

Aunt Gwen came over to put her hand on Mollie's shoulder. ''Mollie, honey, I have to admit, I have doubts about Henry's choice for son-in-law. But Henry felt a common bond with Zach. They both grew up poor in the city. They both lost their mothers at an early age—''

''Zach's mother is dead?''

''Remember the summer you stayed with Henry and me? Remember how Zach treated you badly?''

''Do I!''

''None of us knew it at the time—the Kincannons tend to be close-mouthed about personal matters—but Mary Kincannon was dying that summer. That's why George brought Zach along wherever he worked, to keep an eye on him. Apparently Zach was taking out on you the grief and frustration any child would feel over seeing his mother die by degrees.''

''Oh.'' In that moment, Mollie's view of Zach widened. ''What did she die from?''

''I'm not sure. But once Henry found out what the Kinncannons were going through, he kind of took Zach under his wing.''

''Is that why Zach says he owes you? Because Uncle Henry was good to him?''

Aunt Gwen turned away. She fidgeted some more

with the window shade. ''Uh, actually, it's a little more than that.''

''Such as?''

''Well, after Mary died, and Zach left home, George Kincannon just kind of . . . went to pieces. He started drinking. And he couldn't stop. By the time Henry convinced him to join AA, he'd lost most of his business. Henry paid off the worst of his bills. It added up!''

''Zach didn't know about this?''

''He didn't know George was overcoming a drinking problem until a few months ago. When he got out of the service.''

''What about the debt?''

''That was between George and Henry. George vowed to repay it if it took the rest of his life.''

''So how did Zach find out?''

Aunt Gwen hesitated. Color rose in her face. ''I told him,'' she said quietly.

Mollie was shocked. To break Henry and George's confidence . . .

''Oh, I know,'' Aunt Gwen went on quickly. ''It's not exactly noble. But I had to find some excuse to bring Zach and Sloan together. When George said the Indian Prairie project was more than he could handle— there it was! A gift from heaven! I asked for repayment from Zach—in labor, not money.''

Mollie stood up, agitated. ''Aunt Gwen, how can you use Zach that way? It's not right—''

''Not right to put Zach in the way of a beautiful wife and a fine fortune?''

Mollie's disquiet increased. ''But he and Sloan— I've been around her less than two hours—she's a snob!''

''Oh, you're right. She won't be impressed by the fact Zach is self-reliant and honest and all that good stuff.'' Aunt Gwen's smile was a bit crafty. ''But Zach is handsome; Zach is intelligent. What Zach is *not* is . . . entirely civilized—''

At Mollie's quick frown, Aunt Gwen hurried on. ''I mean, he lives by—I suppose you'd say—a freer set of rules than most of us do. Not motivated by money. Maybe it has something to do with his Indian blood.''

''*What* Indian blood?''

''One of his grandmothers, or some ancestor, was Native American.''

Mollie blew out an impatient breath. ''And he was pumping *me* for Indian history? Making a fool out of me?''

Aunt Gwen smiled. ''I've always heard Indians have a sly sense of humor. Whatever, the fact he's not impressed by wealth will be a novelty to Sloan. Add to that the obvious disenchantment between Zach and me, and voilà, she'll find him irresistible!''

Mollie shook her head in a violent negative. ''I don't like this.''

Aunt Gwen held out her hands. ''Do you see a gun? All I'm doing is putting the two together. All I'm asking of you is to get along with both of them, keep them here until they have a chance to bond.''

''If Zach ever finds out about this—this scheme . . .''

''And how will he find out? This 'scheme' is known only to me. And *you*.''

A direct challenge to Mollie's loyalty . . .

''Mollie.'' Aunt Gwen came close and took her niece's hand. ''If Sloan thought *I* was trying to promote anything between her and Zach, it would be the kiss of death. But if *you* encouraged the match . . .''

Mollie's hands knotted. ''I don't know what to say.''

''What is there to say but 'yes'? If the relationship between Zach and Sloan takes, you'll have benefited both. Immensely. If it doesn't . . .'' Sudden tears sparkled in Aunt Gwen's eyes. ''Mollie, I loved Henry Harris.'' Her tone grew pleading. ''His plan for Indian Prairie was more generous, more high-minded, than I'd ever devise. I know you want the farm to succeed—it's your job, after all. And Henry's hopes for Sloan? I will do whatever I have to do to see them achieved. So I'm begging you, Mollie—help me.''

Mollie felt very strange. She did want to help her aunt; she did want Indian Prairie Farm to live up to Uncle Henry's hopes; and she did want to run this business—oh, how she wanted that! But was it right to play with others' lives to get all this?

''I-I can't see Zach falling for such a stuck-up girl.''

Aunt Gwen pushed back the thick, soft, auburn curls from Mollie's forehead. ''Mollie,'' she said tenderly, ''didn't I tell you Henry was smart about everything except Sloan? I wouldn't bet Zach will catch on any faster.''

Mollie swallowed hard. There was so much sorrow in her aunt's gaze. ''I—I'll do what I can, Aunt Gwen,'' she stammered. She nearly choked on the words.

Mollie's day was ruined. She couldn't decide the ethics of Aunt Gwen's plan. She couldn't shake her disquiet over Zach and Sloan falling in love. . . .

No! Aunt Gwen had to be wrong. Except that, divorced once and widowed twice, Aunt Gwen surely knew a lot more about men than Mollie ever would. Still, this plan to trap Zach—it just didn't feel right. She tried to reason it through, but every time she got to ''I'm begging you, Mollie—help me!'' her mind just shut off.

Late in the afternoon, Mollie trudged up to her room to freshen up for dinner. While she showered, she thought about Sloan's good looks, about the ease with which she could turn seductive. And about how Zach had responded to her so far.

Mollie stepped into clean tan pants and a soft green shirt. Yuck! The outfit had all the appeal of an old dishrag. Yesterday she'd felt feminine and pretty because two young men were vying for her attention. Now nothing was right. Her hair? Nobody wore long curly hair anymore—nobody stylish, at least. And her figure . . .

She left her room to see herself in the full-length hall mirror. ''U-g-g-h!'' The rear view made her look humongous!

''What's the matter? You don't like healthy?''

Mollie's eyes flew from her reflection to the other, teasing gaze meeting hers in the mirror.

Zach leaned against a bedroom doorway, a roll of electrical wire in his hand. His white grin gleamed. ''Don't worry. Wingate thinks you're a dish.''

''You think he looks at me the way you look at Sloan?''

Zach's brows knitted as he shrugged. ''She's easy to notice, all right.''

A wave of plain old unadulterated jealousy swept Mollie. ''Isn't she, though!'' she hissed. She felt so angry, so resentful for the mental turmoil she was experiencing. She wanted to punish Zach for ... for something.

"You know," she charged, "it wasn't very nice of you to let me go on about Ind—Native Americans. Why didn't you tell me you were one of them?"

Zach's grin didn't stop. "Go ahead—say 'Indian.' It's a lot handier than 'Native American.' "

"You know what I mean!"

"It goes back six generations. What's that make me? About one-thirty-secondth Kickapoo?" He came closer, searching her eyes through his grin. "And frankly, my dear, I didn't think you gave a noodle."

"You didn't tell me about the Marines, or college, or ... anything about yourself."

"When did you ask?"

The quiet question shot Molly down in mid-rant. She sputtered a second, her emotions on a seesaw. Then she whipped past Zach to escape down the stairs.

Chapter Six

This was fast becoming the longest weekend of Mollie's life. She tried to convince herself it was fine that Sloan took such an interest in the intricacies of rewiring an old house, or the repairing of plaster on fresh-stripped walls. That she hung around Zach, her lovely lips glistening in a perpetual half-smile. That she thought everything he did was clever, everything he said was funny or important—even though Mollie figured the real attraction was Zach's smooth muscles working beneath his T-shirts. And the friendliness of his grin when he accepted the sodas and snacks Sloan brought him at frequent intervals. Aunt Gwen gave Mollie a thumbs-up as they viewed one such episode from the distance.

But with everybody else, Sloan was a fingernail on a blackboard. A veritable reservoir of sly digs and snobby put-downs.

I have to keep cool; I have to keep cool, Mollie warned herself every time Sloan hit a nerve. *The stakes are high: I have to keep focused on them.*

Sunday morning when Mollie and Aunt Gwen returned from church, Todd met them outside the house. ''I've got a couple of horses saddled up for a ride before I go back to Chicago. Star and Junior.''

''Oh.'' Mollie hesitated. ''I don't know about Junior. So far, I'm the only one who's ridden him, and it wasn't easy.''

''Go put your jeans on, and leave Junior to me.''

''Yes, Mollie,'' Aunt Gwen put in. ''You and Todd should take the opportunity to get better acquainted.''

Mollie felt a pinprick of annoyance. Aunt Gwen was a little obvious.

''Okay, Todd,'' she said. ''But don't blame me if you come back carrying Junior instead of the other way around.''

By the time Mollie returned to the farmyard, Todd had Star and Junior waiting. He helped Mollie mount.

Junior was doing some pawing and snorting. The whites of his eyes showed as Todd prepared to vault into the saddle. Mollie held her breath.

''Todd—'' she warned.

''Don't worry, Mollie—''

Just as Todd swung into the saddle—*Br-a-a-ckkkk-ack-ack!* The Harley charged aggressively down the lane, toward the house. Star danced; Junior reared, shied, bucked, and put on a general demonstration of a horse in terror. A smart rein-lashing got him back under Todd's control. Star gave Junior a disdainful snort that said, ''Dunce!''

The Harley swerved in a smooth circle to halt in front of Mollie and Todd. Zach was driving and behind him rode Sloan, her slim hands clutched around his waist.

Zach pushed up the goggles he was wearing. He nodded toward Todd, still having his hands full with Junior. ''Hey—sorry to cause the disturbance,'' he said. He didn't look all that sorry.

Mollie felt a peevish twist at sight of Sloan and Zach together. ''I've got a suggestion. Put that toy in the garage and leave it there before you kill somebody!''

''No way!''

The exclamation came from Sloan. Her eyes sparkled and her tanned face glowed with excitement. ''You can take me out on it any time, Zach!''

Zach shut off the motor. Sloan's hands stayed at his waist as he balanced the bike with his long, be-jeaned legs. She, as usual, had on shorts and sandals. Her only concession to the slight chill in the air was an oversized Radcliffe sweatshirt.

Todd, not to be out-cooled by Zach, forced Junior to step toward the Harley. ''You're a Cliffie?'' he asked Sloan with a casual gesture toward the shirt.

''Um-hmm,'' Sloan replied lazily. ''A senior. If I decide to go back.''

''There's a question?'' Todd pursued.

Sloan shrugged. ''Radcliffe's no big deal.''

Not if you've got a rich family paying the freight, Mollie thought, remembering the financial scramble her parents had made to help her through state university.

''Who knows?'' Sloan continued, ''I might stay here and take up ranching. Or—''

Mollie was sure Sloan's hands tightened ever so slightly on Zach's waist.

''Something,'' Sloan finished.

Color darkened under Zach's cheekbones.

A sharp-edged reply spun out of Mollie. ''We don't have ranches in Illinois. This is Indian Prairie *Farm!*''

''Ex-cu-u-se me.'' Sloan's laugh was dismissive. ''Zach, are you going to let me drive the Harley now?''

''Uh, you need a helmet. And you're a novice.''

"I learn fast."

Zach didn't say anything. He also didn't move off the driver's seat.

"I hope you have good insurance, Zach," Mollie said.

Sloan frowned. "Look, I say it here in front of witnesses: Zachary Kincannon is not responsible if I wipe out on the Harley. Is that good enough for you?" she inquired insolently of Mollie.

Mollie's face reddened with the effort to keep calm. But Zach saved her a reply.

"Hang it up, Sloan," he said good-naturedly. "I'm drivin'." He pumped the kick pedal a couple of times to prime the carburator, then gave the manly stomp that jabbed the Harley to life.

Sloan didn't argue. A small, admiring smile curled her lips as the Harley roared back down the lane and turned onto the main road.

"Don't let her get to you."

Mollie turned to Todd's amused gaze. "That's easy for you to say. You're not threatened with a whole summer of Sloan."

Todd continued gazing at her, still smiling. "Which bothers you more? A summer with Sloan, or a summer with Sloan hanging onto Kincannon?"

Mollie flushed again. "It's none of my business what Zach and Sloan do—as long as they get out from under my feet while they do it!"

Todd chuckled. "That's the spirit!"

Thunder growled in the distance. Dark clouds rolled low on the horizon. Todd urged Junior close to Star. His free hand glided swift and sure to cup Mollie's chin. "Mollie—"

Her heart wobbled with mixed feelings. Todd was a long way from repulsive, but . . . did she want him to touch her?

"There's—a storm coming," she stammered. "Maybe we should forget the ride."

"You're scared?" His half-grin was mocking.

It took a second for Mollie to corral her conflicting responses. "Of lightning, yes."

He shrugged and dropped his hand. "Okay. I'll take a rain check. Saturday night?"

"You're coming back to Indian Prairie?"

"Every chance I get. I know some great places over in the Quad Cities. How about dinner and—whatever?"

Mollie laughed nervously. "Dinner, yes. Whatever?" She lifted her shoulders. "Depends on whatever 'whatever' turns out to be."

Todd's laughter was full—and assured—as they rode the horses back to the barn.

Thunder still rumbled in the background as Mollie slogged across a sodden farmyard. She'd just finished the evening chores, her clothes were wet, and she was chilled to the bone. Aunt Gwen, Sloan, and Todd had left Indian Prairie in the late afternoon. Mollie looked forward to a hot shower, a light meal, and a quiet evening in her room.

She stopped suddenly, sniffing the wind. She glanced at the house roof. Smoke was pouring from the fireplace chimney.

Mollie hurried into the house. In the lounge, Zach knelt on one knee before the pale red brick fireplace, poking a small blaze into a larger one.

He turned toward Mollie. ''I'm checking out the fireplace. It wouldn't be funny to get all the new paint and paper on, then find out the chimney's clogged.''

''Looks like it's working okay.'' Mollie came to the fireside and spread her hands to the blaze. ''Wow! That heat feels good.''

Zach rose, grinning lopsidedly. ''Your love doesn't keep you warm?''

''It might, if it existed,'' Mollie came back lightly.

''Didn't I hear Todd say something before he left about a big date Saturday night?''

''So?''

''He's driving a hundred and thirty miles just to take you out for dinner? Come on, Mollie.''

Mollie was too tired to bandy words. ''I'm going to get out of these wet clothes,'' she announced.

A shower and clean, warm sweats made her feel better. A trip to the kitchen and a few sips of hot, black tea improved her disposition even further. Now, if she could just curl up in front of the fireplace . . .

On an impulse, she took the teapot and another cup into the lounge.

Zach was stretched out on the sofa.

''Care to join me in a cup of hot tea?''

Zach propped himself on an elbow. ''A hot *tub* would be more fun, but if tea's all you're offering—''

Mollie allowed a small smile. ''It is. I'm surprised you drink the stuff.''

''I don't, usually.''

''Neither do I. But my mom used to make it for me when I was out of sorts.''

His eyes left hers for a second. ''Yeah? So did mine.''

"Oh." Mollie wasn't sure what to say. "I . . . didn't know till yesterday that your mother, uh—"

"Is dead?" Zach supplied.

For a second Mollie glimpsed in his eyes silent love, and pain. "I'm sorry, Zach."

He sat up slowly and motioned her to join him on the only seat in the room. "So am I."

Mollie sat, poured him his tea, then set the tray on the floor in front of them. "Why did she die? If you want to talk about it . . ."

Zach spoke quietly. "She had rheumatic fever when she was a little kid. But it wasn't diagnosed before it did permanent heart damage. So when she got a virus that penicillin would handle for most of us, for her . . . it was too much."

The tiny break in Zach's husky voice was so un-expected. It touched Mollie to the quick. She took a sip of tea, trying to think of a way to get things on lighter ground. She blurted, "Well, what about the rest of your family? Where did you get your Indian blood?"

Zach changed gears, too. A teasing glint returned to his eyes. "Do you really want to know?"

Mollie laughed in relief. "I really want to know."

"In the early 1800s, a settler up in Wisconsin came upon a Kickapoo Indian tribe dying of smallpox. He did what he could, then took a newborn Indian girl home to his wife. They raised her right along with their other kids. And eventually my great-somethin' grandfather, Callum Kincannon—"

" 'Callum?' He wasn't a little bit Scottish, was he?"

"Just a tad. Anyway, Callum came tramping through on a fur trade run, met Small Dove—that was great-something-Grandma—and bingo, they were married within a week.''

''Fast work!''

Zach grinned. ''When a Kincannon finds his woman, he doesn't waste time.''

Mollie could believe that. ''That's a fascinating story. How do you feel about your Native American background?''

''Comfortable.''

''A lot of injustices were done the Indians.''

''Right.''

''So, are you into Native American causes?''

Zach didn't say anything for a second. Then: ''I love my heritage—all of it. But after you've been a few places where people are tearing one another up over tribal fights that started a thousand years back—'' He stared into the fire. ''You get leery of where 'ethnic pride' can take you.''

After a pause, Mollie said, ''I was surprised when Aunt Gwen told me you'd been in the Marines. I can't imagine you liking all that regulation.''

Zach looked back at Mollie, and his tone lightened. ''I didn't. But I saw the reason for it. Once I got out, I swore I'd map out my own life from here on in.''

Aunt Gwen's agenda for Zach and Sloan? Mollie wished she'd never agreed to it. Never even heard of it.

She took refuge in a long sip of tea, then sank back against the soft leather cushions.

''Tired?'' Zach asked in a gentler tone. He took her empty teacup out of her hands and set it on the floor.

Mollie sighed. A little pampering was just what she needed. ''Yes! Being nice to—uh—everybody all weekend just wore me out.''

Zach chuckled. "How's it going to work when you have to be nice all week to paying guests?"

"I don't know," Mollie murmured, shutting her eyes. "Maybe I'll just stay with the horses."

"I thought you handled the weekend real well, Mollie. Considering how bad you wanted to slug Sloan."

Mollie's eyes flew open and she sat up. "I did not! I just didn't like—"

Zach's laughter rolled over her until she grinned in return. "You love it, don't you, Zach," Mollie jokingly accused, "the way Ms. East Coast Charm cuts me up!"

Chuckling, Zach stretched his long legs in front of him and rested his head on the sofa back. "Hey, it keeps you off my back!"

For Mollie the tensions of the weekend began to dissolve. She was warm and cozy. She liked the comforting presence of the man beside her. Aunt Gwen was gone, Todd was gone, and best of all, Sloan was gone. At least temporarily. Maybe fate would intervene; maybe Sloan wouldn't come back.

She watched the firelight play off Zach's manly profile. Who would have thought he could be so easy to be around? So enjoyable to be around?

"Well, I'll just tell you, Zachary," she murmured. "If—or when—Sloan comes back, I'm gonna be so nice to her, it'll make you sick!"

The front door slammed. Quick, light steps crossed from the hall to the lounge.

"Guess what?"

Mollie and Zach jerked toward the voice from the doorway. Mollie's heart sank.

"I'm back."

It was Sloan.

Chapter Seven

‘‘Can we talk?’’

Dee blew back the hair tendril tickling her forehead as she made her request of Mollie.

‘‘Sure. What is it?’’

‘‘Three guesses and the first two don't count.’’

Mollie had a sinking feeling as she and Dee took seats across from each other at the picnic table.

‘‘What's she done now?’’

Dee took a deep breath. ‘‘This morning she informed me that Ray and I should 'take our lunch in the kitchen'—I think that was her eloquent phrase. In other words, no serfs in the dining room!’’

Mollie slapped her coffee mug to the table, spilling hot contents on her knee. ‘‘Ouch!’’ She hastily brushed at her knee. ‘‘That takes the cake! First it's the meals—too heavy, too hurried, too beef-and-porky. Then it's her room, not big enough. Now it's you and Ray?’’

‘‘What I want to know is how come she's here on Thursday when she was supposed to leave on Sunday?’’

Mollie chuckled. Grimly. ‘‘She and Aunt Gwen did leave. But they caught up with Todd at a gas station in Shawano, and Aunt Gwen said she might just as well go back to Chicago with him so that Sloan could come back here.’’

"Lucky, lucky us."

"Yeah." Mollie sipped morosely at her coffee. The past four days had been one confrontation after another with Sloan. The girl had the business sense of a sulky cat. But she insisted on second-guessing every decision Mollie made.

"She's been on the phone with Todd every day," Mollie said, "with one extravagant suggestion after another for renovating this house. Right over my head, you know—I'm only the one who's got to make this place pay for itself."

"Where is Her Royal Highness this morning?"

"Went to the Quad Cities, clothes shopping."

"Good!" Dee said. "Maybe she'll pick up enough to cover her body! Do you know, she had the nerve to ask me to do her personal laundry? On a daily basis?"

"And you said—?"

" 'The washer and dryer are in the basement. Feel free.' "

Mollie laughed.

"I've got to start lunch, Mollie," Dee said, rising. "I hate to lay this on you when you've got so much to do, but I swear, if that girl makes one more crack about my meals, I'm gonna—" Dee left her threat hanging.

"I'll take care of it," Mollie promised. She finished her coffee, dreading the return of Sloan. It shouldn't be long. Sloan wouldn't stay away from Zach for any length of time.

Mollie sighed. It wasn't her nature to enjoy bad relations. With anybody. She had to get a grip on her animosity toward Sloan. The girl must have *some* good qualities. Even a stopped clock was right twice a day. . . .

The regulars at Indian Prairie were just sitting down to lunch when Sloan's Saab whipped into the farmyard. They waited a few minutes for her to saunter into the house with a couple of loaded shopping bags. She stashed them by the hall staircase and took her place—beside Zach, of course—at the table.

''Looks like you bought out the shopping mall,'' Ray commented with a grin. ''Don't get any ideas, Dee.''

Sloan's reaction was a barely-there smile.

''You weren't gone very long,'' Mollie remarked to fill the rather awkward silence that followed.

Sloan's brow raised. ''How long could it take? The shopping's not exactly Saks.''

Mollie pushed down her annoyance. She began to pass bowls and platters.

Everyone but Sloan took generous servings. She took one tiny slice of beef, then worried it with her knife and fork—which she used European-style—but didn't actually take a bite. ''Isn't there a thing, a thermometer, you can use to prevent overcooking meat? If I have to eat beef, I prefer it rare. Very rare.''

Dee gave her own slice of tender roast a vicious slash of the knife. But her answer came with forced sweetness. ''Next time, I'll take your portion out early.''

Ray, ever good-natured, contemplated his plate. ''Um-hmm! Roast beef, mashed potatoes, gravy, scalloped corn—does it get any better?''

Sloan laid down her fork. ''Does it get any more Midwestern?''

The unvarnished scorn in her voice set Mollie's

trouble antenna aquiver. And Dee? For a moment, Mollie thought Dee was going to dump her plate right over Sloan's sarcastic head.

Zach's eyes went black. Deliberately he lifted a forkful of beef to his mouth, chewed judiciously, then swallowed. "If Midwestern means delicious," he drawled, dangerously soft, "then the answer is 'no.' " He looked straight at Dee. "Your cooking is great, Dee. I never ate better."

Mollie could have kissed him. Dee's frown disappeared in an appreciative smile.

Sloan's full lips pulled into a pout. She took a few sips of iced tea, then excused herself from the table.

Nobody spoke until Sloan disappeared up the staircase. Then the conversation, like relief, began to flow. Mollie made up her mind she'd have to speak to Sloan immediately. Otherwise Indian Prairie would probably be looking for another chief cook and bottle washer.

Consequently, once lunch was over, Mollie went upstairs. She paused outside Sloan's closed door, searching her brain for the right thing to say. Well, there was nothing to do but beard the lion.

Mollie knocked.

"Yes?"

"It's me, Mollie. Could I see you for a minute, Sloan?"

There was a pause, then, "Come in."

Sloan lay across her unmade bed, reading a magazine. Scattered on the floor were a couple of pairs of new Levi's and some T-shirts. Black T-shirts. Wellington boots, like the ones Zach often wore, sprawled out of a box.

Sloan barely acknowledcdcd Mollie's presence.

Mollie wasn't one to dance around a subject.

"Sloan, if you're going to be around Indian Prairie for a while, there are some ground rules we need to go over."

Slowly Sloan turned onto her side. She regarded Mollie coolly. "I couldn't agree more."

Mollie was taken aback. "Well, good. To start with—"

Sloan threw the magazine to the floor and sat up on the bed. "To start, I want a new menu for lunch, which will be at one o'clock, and dinner, which will be at eight. I want lots of seafood, lots of fresh fruits and vegetables—"

"Sloan," Mollie broke in, "people doing hard physical labor need a big meal at noon. They can't operate on a lettuce leaf and a fish flake. Which brings me to the high price of seafood. I love it, too, but no way will the Indian Prairie budget stretch to cover shrimp and lobster for our hearty crew."

"Which brings *me,*" Sloan said, "to the totally ludicrous dining arrangements around here. From now on, I expect the Joneses—and any other servants—to eat in the kitchen. The dining room is off-limits."

Mollie controlled an instant spurt of anger. "I don't think you understand, Sloan. Out here, we don't have servants. We have hired help. With the emphasis on *help*. If we don't have Dee in charge of the household and Ray handling the farmwork, Indian Prairie's gonna be in a lot of trouble."

Sloan slid off the bed to stand face-to-face with Mollie. "This is my property. I can always get somebody else to work here."

Mollie shook her head no. "It's your property, but it's not under your control."

"Yet."

"Yet," Mollie agreed. "But until it is, I'm managing Indian Prairie. And I say we all treat each other decently. We all do our share. And we all eat together."

Sloan's eyes snapped. "I'll take my meals in my room!"

"Fine. You can fill your plate in the kitchen and take it anywhere you please."

For once, Sloan didn't have a fast comeback. Her mouth opened, then closed in a stubborn line.

Mollie's shoulders rose in a pleading gesture. "Sloan, for the success of this place, let's cooperate. Your father had a good idea. Let's make it work."

Sloan's face clouded. "I have ideas, too. I don't expect to have them ruined by a cook and a local farmer. Maybe you're afraid to put Dee in her place, but I'm not."

Oh, brother! Sloan had to be headed off from that precipice! Mollie grabbed the first verbal weapon that came to mind. "Maybe you'd better run that idea past Zach."

Sloan eyed her suspiciously. "Why?"

"Because Zach is like Dee and Ray and me—a worker. A Midwesterner."

Sloan turned away. "Zach," she said in a low, positive voice, "isn't like anybody else. He's special." Defiantly, she met Mollie's gaze. "If you can't see that, you're blind."

So. Over an inexplicable wincing of the heart, Mollie said quietly, "Just give my advice a chance."

Sloan didn't reply.

Mollie started to leave the room.

"Oh, by the way," Sloan said, "Zach and I won't be here for dinner tonight."

Mollie turned in surprise. ''No?''

Sloan shook her head, a confident smile returning to her face. ''We're going to the Cities. I heard about an interesting little bistro when I was shopping this morning. Down along the Mississippi. Specializes in Creole, and New Orleans jazz.''

''Does Zach know about this?'' Mollie asked, trying to sound offhand.

Sloan plucked a bikini swimsuit from a Victoria's Secret bag. She held it up to the light, pretending to examine it critically. ''He'll go.'' She turned to face Mollie again. ''Don't you think?''

Mollie dabbed at her steaming face with a tissue. The weather, typical for Illinois, had made a U-turn overnight from cool to unseasonably warm. ''You think your brother still wants a job here?'' she inquired of Dee.

Dee settled herself under the steering wheel of her ancient Camaro. ''Ralphie wants a job. More important,'' she emphasized, ''Ray and I want him to have a job. Mom and Dad don't want him bopping around the Cities all summer while they're at work, and we're glad to help out. But he's got to have something constructive to do.''

Mollie leaned through the window to talk to her helper. ''But will he think mucking out a horse barn or mowing the lawn is 'constructive?' Teenagers can be a mighty picky lot.''

''Pick, schmick! The kid's got to work. And like Ray says, running big farm machinery is no place for a fourteen-year-old city dude to start. So he can run a shovel and pitchfork first.''

Mollie laughed. ''Okay. When's school out?''

"The last of May."

Mollie mopped her brow again. "I hope I can last that long. It's been a while since I did all that shoveling, too."

Dee thought for a second. "Mom and Dad and Ralphie are coming over for dinner tonight. How about if Ralphie stays the weekend and tries out with you? You don't have to pay him till you see if he can handle the job."

"Sounds good to me. Send him over in the morning. About six-thirty."

"Will do." Dee started the car. "Oh—" She leaned out the window. "And don't be put off by Ralphie's looks. He's basically a good kid. Just looks . . . funny."

Dee put the car in gear and rolled down the driveway before Mollie could get her definition of "looks . . . funny."

Mollie wandered over to the pasture gate and leaned against it. It didn't take Star long to come trotting in expectation of the handful of tender grass Mollie offered her.

"The grass is always greener?"

Mollie turned toward Zach's remark. Her heart skipped a beat. Obviously Sloan had had her way, and they were going out. He had on loose gray cotton pants and a white cotton shirt, full sleeves rolled to mid-forearm. His hair, always shining clean, was banded at the nape of his neck. The simplest clothes, but he looked great in them.

"Well, Mr. Kincannon," Mollie said over a slight catch in her throat, "you clean up pretty good. Aren't you afraid you'll get jambalaya on that hot shirt?"

Zach laughed easily. "I'll tie on a bib." He had

two cans of soda in his hand. He handed one to Mollie. "I've got a message for you."

Mollie looked her inquiry.

"Todd Wingate just called. Said to remind you he'd pick you up about six tomorrow night."

Mollie popped the top of her soda can. Six would rush her, but thank goodness she'd have Ralphie to help with the chores tomorrow night. "Thanks for the message. And the pop," she added as she brushed back the hair hanging warm around her forehead.

"Sure. Maybe I can tell you where to get some good jambalaya tomorrow night."

Mollie's smile was dry. "Actually, I was thinking more of filet. Or pork chops. You know—something Midwestern."

Zach leaned to pick a handful of grass. He offered it to Star. "She's just a kid, you know," he remarked quietly.

"Kid? She's twenty. What are you, fifty?"

"I'm twenty-four. But in terms of what Sloan knows about real life—" He lifted his shoulders. "Exclusive girls' schools and fancy stores—that's not where it's at."

"Something—or somebody—has sure taught her to expect everything to go her way."

Zach began to stroke Star's nose.

"Watch your fingers," Mollie warned automatically. "Sometimes horses bite."

Zach heeded her warning. "Nobody has everything their way all the time," he said thoughtfully. He continued to pet Star, higher on her face.

"Maybe not. Anyway, thanks for coming to the defense of Dee's roast beef. She's just about had it with Ms. Snobella."

Zach grinned and shook his head. "So Sloan's OD'd on ritzy ideas? Give her time; she'll grow out of it."

Mollie smiled over a desire to snap. "I wonder whether you'd be so tolerant if Sloan were dumb and ugly!"

Zach laughed again, flicking back a curl from Mollie's hot forehead. "You think Wingate's hanging around you because you're so old and wise?"

Mollie's lips screwed into an ironic grin. "It's my money. And my convertible. And my big appetite for fun and games."

Zach laughed aloud. "Where's all that sweetness toward Sloan you promised the other night? You mad because I'm going out with her tonight?"

"In your dreams!" Mollie joked. "Where's all your independence? She's maneuvering you right around her little finger."

"I've got no apologies if a pretty girl with a lot of dough wants to take me out to repay a favor."

"Favor?" The word caught Mollie's ear. "What does she owe you for?"

"Teaching her to ride the Harley."

"How sweet!"

Zach moved away from the gate. "Hey, I'll give you lessons any time you want 'em."

"No thanks." Mollie started to walk away.

Zach strode up beside her. "Now who's being a snob?"

"Snob? Just because I want to keep my brain in my skull?"

"Like a horse never throws you? I saw old Junior at work."

The two leaned on either side of the picnic table. Zach took a long swig of soda.

Sloan came out the kitchen door, her golden tan beautifully set off by a short white skirt, white bare midriff top, and white strappy sandals. She carried a tray with two chilled glasses and two bottles of beer. She set the tray on the table, ignoring Mollie, and took the soda can from Zach's hand.

"How about a real drink, Zach?" Sloan twirled a bottle to show him the label. "Imported, straight from Germany. I think you'll like it."

Zach's enthusiasm was unnoticeable. But under Sloan's urging, he poured two glasses of beer. He pushed one glass toward Mollie, the other toward Sloan. "Drink up, ladies."

Sloan frowned, then saw the light—she thought. She handed Zach the other bottle of beer. "I might have known, you like yours straight from the bottle."

Zach shook his head no.

Mollie guessed what was behind his refusal, but Sloan got a pouty look.

"What's the matter? You don't like German beer?"

"I just don't do booze," Zach replied matter-of-factly.

"Don't do—" Sloan looked incredulous. "You don't drink anything? Not even *beer?*"

Zach's smile didn't extend to his eyes. "I don't need it," he said quietly, "so I don't do it."

Mollie took a swift sip of the dark brew. "It's very good," she assured Sloan, taking another quick sip. Actually, she didn't much like it. Too malty, or something.

Sloan's mouth pulled down even further.

Zach grinned. ''Hey—it's no big deal. You want to have fun? I can do it with or without the juice.''

A slow, reluctant smile curled in Sloan's face. Her eyes took on a sparkle. ''I'll bet you can!''

She pulled car keys from her tiny shoulder bag and dangled them enticingly in front of Zach. ''Wanta go by bike? Or drive my car?''

Zach took the keys. He grinned down at Sloan mischievously. ''I feel humble tonight. Let's take the car.''

Chapter Eight

*I*s this a new level in weird, or have I just been out
of high school too long?

Mollie stared at the yawning kid standing in front
of her. Ralphie Van Wass was fourteen and gangly.
He had shoulder-length brown hair. On one side. The
left side of his head was cropped to near extinction.
Below the Walkman earphone piping rap into his left
ear dangled a long silver earring. Baggy denim shorts,
a humongous plaid shirt, and combat-type boots completed his ensemble.

"So, Ralphie," Mollie began tentatively. No wonder Dee had dumped her brother and sped away like
the wind. "You want to learn the horse trade?"

Ralphie tongued a wad of gum from one cheek to
the other. "I guess so."

"Have you ever been around horses? Or ridden
one?"

Ralphie shrugged. "I've, you know, ridden ponies
at the Fun Park. That's about it."

That's about it. Mollie ran a hand over her long
French braid. What had Dee saddled her with?

"Well, I guess the only way to find out if you can
handle the job is to try it, right? Let's go to the barn,
and I'll show you the morning routine."

Ralphie nodded a brief okay.

"Oh—better leave your Walkman on the picnic table. You'll need to listen with both ears."

"Can I put it in the house? Someone might, you know, rip it off out here."

"Uh, sure."

Once in the barn, Mollie began to show Ralphie the general layout. "What's that wagon in the middle of the barn?" Ralphie wanted to know. "Do the horses pull it?"

Mollie grinned. "That's called the 'honey wagon,' Ralphie," she explained. "That's where you throw the manure and dirty straw every day. Then Ray comes over and hauls it away with a tractor for fertilizer."

"Ya have to clean this floor every *day?*" Ralphie didn't look happy about that.

"Yes, you do, Ralphie," Mollie said, serious. "Standing in muck can literally rot away a horse's hooves. Besides that, flies breed like crazy in manure."

Ralphie's face remained expressionless, but Mollie had the feeling he was about ready to bail out. She plowed ahead, showing him how to mix rations, which, to her surprise, he picked up right away. Then she whistled in the herd, and while it chomped on breakfast, Ralphie got a lesson in brushing coats and checking hooves.

She started him with gentle old Pet, whose idea of violence was shuddering flies off her coat. Mollie could tell Ralphie was a bit hesitant about getting so close to good-sized horses, but she counted on his male bravado to force him on.

It worked. By the time he'd finished grooming Pet, Ralphie was sweating a little, but he seemed to like the feel of a warm, silky coat under his hands.

By nine o'clock, the morning chores were done, and Mollie invited Ralphie to the picnic table for a snack break. The Harley, of course, was at its usual resting place under the apple tree.

"Hey!" Ralphie forgot some of his cool as he walked over to inspect the powerful old machine. "This yours?"

Mollie grinned wryly. "Unh-unh. I stick to horses and pickups."

"Man!" Ralphie studied the cycle. "Can I—?" He indicated he'd like to try the seat.

"I guess so. Just don't mess with anything."

Ralphie slid onto the seat. His eyes shone. "I bet this dude really blasts!" he muttered.

Just then Zach came around the corner of the house carrying a couple of buckets of paint. He stopped short at the sight of Ralphie perched on the Harley.

"Uh—" Ralphie looked up at the tall man uncertainly. "Just . . . checkin' this out," he offered lamely.

Zach set the paint cans on the table and stood, hands on hips, eyeing the youngster.

"She, uh—" Ralphie pointed to Mollie. "She, you know, said it was okay."

Ralphie broke off in the face of Zach's unwavering stare. Mollie detected a twinkle in Zach's dark eyes.

"Good," Zach said slowly. " 'Cause I wouldn't want to think you were gonna rip off my bike."

"Hey, man—no!" Ralphie slid hastily from the seat.

Zach laughed. "It's cool; I believe you."

Sloan came out of the house with her morning coffee. She had on a set of her new jeans and T-shirts. Her eyes flickered over Mollie, then Ralphie, but her greeting to them was minimal.

''Zach!'' she murmured, sidling up beside him. ''Why didn't you wake me? I want to get started on our project.''

Zach's grin lessened. ''That's got to wait, Sloan. I have to finish painting the walls today.''

Sloan's eyes lit on Ralphie. ''Don't we have a new 'helper?' Can't he do it?''

''I don't know what your project is, Sloan,'' Mollie said, ''but Ralphie's the outdoor man. I've got a full day planned for him.''

Sloan looked stormy. ''The project is very simple. Zach's going to teach me to ride the Harley; I'm going to give him lessons in horsemanship.''

''You ride?'' Mollie queried.

''Of course,'' Sloan answered, as if the question were ridiculous. ''Since I was three.''

Mollie couldn't help nothing, ''I thought you weren't interested in horses, Zach.''

He didn't say anything.

''Anyway, if you do have a spare minute, I wish you'd take the truck into Shawano and pick up some furniture I've paid for at the House of Bargains.''

''They don't deliver?'' Zach asked.

''Hardly. It's a secondhand store. I've got a couple of easy chairs for the lounge waiting for someone to pick them up—''

''Secondhand store?'' Sloan broke in. ''Why are you buying junk like that?''

Mollie gritted against irritation. ''Simple economics. That's what Indian Prairie can afford.''

''Maybe Sloan could drive in and get them?'' Zach suggested.

''The store is run by a woman. She'll need help loading the truck.''

Zach took a long look at Ralphie. "Ralphie, how would you like to develop your biceps? If Mollie can spare you, that is?"

Ralphie shifted weight. "Well, I dunno—"

Mollie wanted the furniture. She also welcomed a rest from "training" Ralphie. "I think that's a good idea. Sloan?"

Sloan looked less than thrilled, but with Zach making the suggestion, what could she say? Within minutes, she and Ralphie were in the truck, and Mollie was giving them directions to the House of Bargains. "Just be sure to be back by three o'clock, Ralphie. We've got some extra chores to do tonight."

And I want to have plenty of time to get ready for my date, she added mentally.

The next few hours flew by. Mollie had myriad things to attend to. One o'clock came; no returnees. Two o'clock . . . three . . .

She went out to the barn. Could Sloan and Ralphie have gotten lost? That didn't seem likely. The road from the farm led directly into Shawano. So what was taking so long?

Mollie began portioning out rations for the herd's afternoon feeding. She eyed the empty manure wagon Ray had just brought back. She hated shovel work. And she preferred not to go creaking and groaning into her date tonight with Todd.

Four o'clock. Mollie brought in the herd, then waited impatiently for them to eat so she could drive them out again and begin cleaning.

Four-thirty. Mollie was beginning to get mad. She turned the herd into the pasture and picked up her shovel. She started scooping.

Five o'clock. Half the stalls were still to be cleared.

Mollie sped to a feverish pace that popped the sweat out on her forehead.

''What's goin' on?''

Zach came into the barn.

Mollie kept shoveling. ''My so-called helper and your so-called kid haven't showed, that's what.''

''Well, can't you just let this go till morning?''

In three short sentences Mollie set Zach straight as to the necessity of clean stalls.

Zach advanced into the barn. ''Gee! One more good reason for Harleys!''

Mollie stopped to lean on her shovel, breathless. ''Don't start with that!''

Zach glanced at his watch. ''It's after five. Hadn't you better start getting ready for your big date?''

Mollie clamped her lips to keep from shouting. As if she wanted to be out here ankle deep in . . .

Zach strode over to her. In one swift movement, he had the shovel in his hands. ''Get out,'' he ordered softly.

It took a second for Mollie to understand. ''Zach, you don't get paid for this—''

''G-e-t o-u-t,'' he commanded gently. ''You don't want to go on a hot date smelling like a horse. Go get pretty.''

''But I won't have time—''

Zach's tough, warm hand came around hers. ''You've got time. When Wingate gets here, I'll keep him entertained till you make your big entrance.''

Mollie looked up into warm, dark eyes. She saw her reflection. She also saw a kindness, a consideration she was beginning to expect in Zach. She swallowed uncertainly.

''Thanks, Zach. I'll . . . make it up to you.''

''You're not the one with making up to do. When those two do get back from town, I will personally flatten their heads into shovels and start scooping! Now, go.'' He gave her a light shove and sent her on her way.

Exactly one hour later, Mollie came out into the farmyard. Everything soap, water, shampoo, cologne, makeup, and a lilac silk halter dress could do for her, they did.

Todd and Zach were bent over the Harley, fiddling with some control or other. They both turned to face Mollie's soft, ''I'm . . . ready.''

Todd's eyes took on an appreciative gleam. ''Nice,'' he murmured. ''Very nice.''

Zach didn't say anything. But his smile was slow and tongue-in-cheek. When Todd's back was turned, Zach gave Mollie the A-okay sign.

Mollie smoothed the brush of lavish auburn curls on her shoulders. As Todd led her toward his car, she twisted slightly to see Zach. ''I'll see you in the morning. Thanks—again.''

From now on, I'm not going to spend so much time in denim and boots, she resolved silently as she and Todd took to the road.

Mollie let out the shriek that had been building since Sloan Harris first set foot on Indian Prairie. ''She *what?*''

''Bought it in the Cities. Put it on down payment, that is.''

It was early Sunday morning. Mollie and Zach stood in the middle of the lounge, surrounded by a roomful of luscious, tasteful, expensive new furniture.

Everything in natural leather, distressed oak, earth tones—Southwest with dollar signs.

"I can't believe this!" The explosion aggravated Mollie's forehead. Last night had been a big night— too late, too much dancing, too much champagne. Now to find Sloan had spent all yesterday afternoon in the Cities running up a national debt . . .

"I thought you'd be real pleased," Zach drawled with irony. "The furniture van pulled in about five minutes after you and Todd left. But it wasn't up to me to tell 'em to take the stuff back."

Mollie was so angry she was beginning to shake. She pivoted and started for the door.

"Where are you going?" Zach's hand on her arm stopped her.

"Upstairs. To have this out with Sloan right now!"

"Hold on. Give yourself time to cool down."

"Zach, I've had it with her! I'm living with a bare-bones budget, and this . . . this *twit* blows it in one afternoon! She's going to get on the phone and tell that furniture store to come get this stuff today!"

"Mollie." Zach's face was serious. "I don't blame you for being mad. But take it easy. Cool down."

Mollie seethed.

"Listen, Mollie—you like to go to church, don't you? Maybe you should do that before you jump on Sloan."

Mollie's jaw set. "The way I feel toward her, I don't trust myself to drive into Shawano. I'd probably wipe out some innocent carload of people!"

Zach was quiet for a second. "I'll go with you."

Mollie looked up at him with surprise. "To church?"

"Sure." Zach grinned slightly. "What's the matter, you think the walls will fall down?"

Mollie's frown slowly dissolved in a reluctant grin. "I just never figured you for a Sunday School boy."

Zach's mouth twitched at the corners. "You never figured me right for much of anything, farm girl."

A week ago—even a day ago—Mollie would have fired at the hated "farm girl" label. But things were different now. Zach might tease, but Zach came through in a pinch.

"Okay," she said. "I'll do the pony chores, then—"

"Un-unh. Ralphie's coming over, remember? I'll get him started on the chores, then we're out of here."

"Ralphie?" Mollie groaned. "Ralphie's probably high-tailed it back to Rock Island by now!"

"I don't think so," Zach said. "We had a talk last night while we cleaned the barn."

"What kind of talk?"

Zach's lips pulled askew. "Let's say Ralphie now understands he doesn't get paid for directing Sloan to every furniture store in the Quad Cities."

By ten, Mollie and Zach were in church. And she had to admit, she felt better after an hour's focus on something bigger than her own concerns. Afterward, Zach suggested they have lunch in a little Main Street restaurant.

Mollie hesitated. "I don't know—I was going to fix lunch for Todd . . . for all of us," she quickly amended.

Zach ended the discussion with "Let 'em eat cornflakes."

Last night, it had been swordfish en papillote at a swank Quad Cities supper club. Today it was roast chicken and accompaniments at the tiny, immaculate Farmer's Inn. Last night Mollie had gazed out at the diamond-bright lights of riverboat casinos plying the Mississippi River. Today she looked through snowy curtains at cars drifting along the plain small-town street, shadowless in the hot midday sun.

Last night, in spite of the exquisite meal, Mollie had left more than half her food on her plate. It wasn't just that Todd was so sophisticated, so sure of himself. Mollie had the feeling he valued her chiefly because she looked so good on his arm. And then when his kisses had turned insistent . . .

"Uh—?"

She snapped back to the present at Zach's soft reminder that laden plates had been set before them, and he was waiting politely for her to pick up her fork.

"Oh!" Mollie colored a little. "Sorry. I spaced out."

Zach grinned but didn't say anything.

Mollie didn't feel hungry. Until she took the first taste of food, that is. It was solidly, totally, Midwesternly delicious. She looked across at Zach; he didn't expect her to be sophisticated. He didn't need her as an expensive decoration. Suddenly she relaxed into an immense appetite.

"You want some of mine?"

Mollie looked up into Zach's laughing eyes. She'd consumed everything but the sprig of parsley on her plate. "Wow—I ate like there was no tomorrow!"

Zach chuckled. "Hey, you're a growing girl."

"Yeah—sideways."

"Sideways . . . frontways . . . what you did for that dress last night—it's all for a good cause."

Mollie laughed. "Thanks. But you won't say that when I'm fat and forty."

Zach took a sip of iced tea. "Fat? So what? And forty—that's a long way off. But I guess we'll get there. Eventually."

"Yeah. Unless the Harley does you in."

"Or Junior tramples you trying to get out the gate." He stopped the waitress to ask for the dessert menu. Over Mollie's protests he placed two orders for raspberry pie with ice cream. Two dips.

When the last lovely, gooey bit of pie à la mode had slid down her throat, Mollie sat back, sighing with repletion. She closed her eyes. "How did you know I needed that sugar binge?" she murmured.

"You're an easy book to read, Ms. Moreau. Just like last night. You had 'I'm gonna die if I miss my date with Todd!' written all over your face."

Mollie opened her eyes. "It wasn't Todd so much," she countered. "I just wanted to get out of jeans for a while. Go somewhere fancy."

"Sure, sure. Todd is smart, good looking, moving up in the world. And he's got big plans for you. Why be defensive about liking him?"

"Who said I like him?"

Zach's eyes were friendly. But wise. "Maybe you like the idea of moving up in the world."

Mollie stirred. The Plan—Uncle Henry's plan for Zach to marry Sloan—popped into Mollie's thoughts. "Well, who would mind that? Under the right circumstances, that is."

"Give me an example."

Mollie squirmed ever so slightly. "Well, obviously, I'll never get rich running Indian Prairie. But if I fell in love with a man who had money, I wouldn't turn it down. Would you?''

''No.''

She leaned forward, earnest. ''Zach, what are your career plans? After you finish at Indian Prairie?''

He considered. ''I'm not sure. I know I don't want to be a suit, running to catch the commuter train every morning. I'm not zeroed in on making it big like Wingate. But I figure one of these days, just the right opportunity will come along. And I'll know what I was looking for.''

Mollie thought of Sloan. ''Maybe opportunity's not a job. Maybe it's a person.''

Zach studied her; his eyes grew dark, unreadable. ''Maybe.''

There was a short silence. Mollie broke it with, ''It's time I got back to the farm to take up the furniture war.''

On the long ride to the farm, Zach suggested, ''Why don't you let me talk to Sloan about returning the furniture? She wants to give me a horseback riding lesson this afternoon.''

Mollie turned to scrutinize his profile. ''Oh, really?''

''Now, what's that for? I'm just trying to give you another chance to be alone with Hot Toddy.''

Mollie laughed. ''You're so thoughtful! Frankly, I'm bushed. I'd just like a couple of hours to myself.''

Zach shrugged. ''Have it your way.'' A mischievous smile curled the corners of his lips. ''I'm just trying to be helpful.''

Mollie laughed again. ''Sure you are.''

The pickup pulled into Indian Prairie just as Todd came out of the house with his duffel bag in hand. He waited beside his car. "Thought maybe you'd left the country," he remarked coolly as Mollie came to his side.

He's miffed because I came down on the "no" side last night, Mollie thought. "I . . . had something important to take care of," she said.

Todd's half-grin was doubting. "Busy, busy, busy! Well, darlin', I've got to motor. I left some plans for possible house renovations on the dining table. Let me know what you think about 'em, and I'll come back to talk."

"You can't go over them now?"

"I'm busy, too, hon." He chucked her under the chin. "Don't worry. I'll make plenty of time for us. When you're ready." He dropped a quick kiss on her lips and slid into his car.

" 'Bye, now," he called over the revved motor. Mollie stepped back as he took off down the drive. She frowned, rubbing the back of her neck.

"I thought maybe you'd got rid of your headache."

She turned toward Zach, lounging beside the truck, a small grin on his face. He tapped his forehead. "The one up here, I mean." He walked over and put a brotherly arm around her shoulder. "Come on, take an aspirin and call Dr. Todd in the morning," he kidded, urging her toward the house.

She managed a single, tired chuckle.

It was late afternoon when Mollie wakened from a deep nap. It took a second for her brain to clear, then she got off her bed and slipped into her pony-chore jeans and shirt. A cup of fresh coffee, and she felt pretty good as she headed across the farmyard.

Which two horses did Sloan and Zach take out? she

wondered. She paused at the pasture gate to check who was missing. *Hmm. Tony and—Star? She took* my *horse out?*

Mollie stalked into the barn, fuming. Zach might not know riding etiquette, but Sloan, experienced equestrienne that she claimed to be, knew better than to ride somebody's private steed without permission. *One more reason to kill her,* Mollie grumbled silently.

The pasture grass was getting close-cropped, Mollie remembered. She'd better start feeding hay along with the usual rations. Accordingly, she climbed the ladder into the hayloft and dragged a bale to the edge of the first of six holes cut in the floor right above the stalls below. She cut the twine with the knife kept stuck in the wall for that purpose. She kicked the bale apart, then stuffed the hay through the hole.

''Dang!'' There were bees in the hayloft; Mollie dodged from one hanging around her too close for comfort. The bee flew off, and she continued dragging bales and stuffing hay. She was halfway through with the last hole, the one above Star and Tony's stalls, when she heard horses clopping into the barn.

''So what do you think of your first ride?'' came in Sloan's sultry tones.

Mollie froze. Of course, she should throw down the last of the hay so Sloan and Zach would know she was right above them. But . . .

Leaning cautiously forward, Mollie could glimpse the scene below through the hay.

Zach dismounted; he rubbed Tony's neck. ''Well, he ain't no Harley!''

Sloan joined his laughter. ''But it's fun, isn't it?'' She walked over to him. Very close. ''You're going to be a wonderful horseman, Zach. You've got a great natural seat.''

He glanced sideways at her. ''Yeah?''

Sloan's laugh was low, sultry. ''That's horse talk for 'You're a born rider.' Here—'' She slid a slim arm past his brawny one. ''Let me show you how to take off the saddle.''

Oh, brother, Mollie thought. *She's about as subtle as a bulldozer!*

Zach chuckled. ''Doesn't it come off the opposite way it went on?''

Move away, you fool! Mollie groused inwardly. *Can't you see she's stalking you?*

Apparently Zach didn't mind being stalked. He exchanged Tony's bridle for a halter while Sloan loosened the saddle girth. ''You know,'' she said, ''we can have a lot of fun this summer. Horseback riding, Harley riding . . . and other stuff.''

''Sure we can—if I have the time. I've got a lot of work to do around here.''

''No.'' Sloan put her hand on the saddle horn. ''You don't. I have plenty of money. I can hire somebody to do your job, and we'll . . . vacation.''

Zach hung the bridle over a peg. He turned back to the beautiful girl leaning against the horse. ''I'm not for sale, Sloan.''

Good for you! Mollie silently cheered.

Sloan's eyelids fluttered down; she was either hurt, or giving a good imitation of it. She turned to Tony and started to lift the saddle off his back.

''I'll do it.'' Zach had raised the saddle about an inch when Sloan brushed lazily at a speck of white dandelion caught in his hair. ''Zach,'' she murmured, ''you seem to do everything so well . . . I wonder—''

She lifted herself to kiss him softly on the lips.

Mollie could see blood come up in Zach's tan cheeks.

Sloan smiled up at him. "Now it's your turn."

Mollie thought she heard some uneasiness in Zach's short laugh. "I don't usually kiss on command."

Sloan's laughter was warm and silky. "It's a request."

Zach hesitated. Then, while Mollie peered from above, a strangling sensation at her throat, he reached for Sloan with one hand, pulling her close for a brief touch on the lips.

Sloan's arms wrapped around his neck. "Come on, you can do better than that!" she teased.

Just then the bee that had bothered Mollie earlier returned. He buzzed her head, then landed on her ear. She gave a wild swat, stepping back, then—*crash!*

The horses reared, and Sloan let out a scream. As the walls spun, Mollie, through a cloud of dust, tried to lift herself from the barn floor.

"What in the—you were *spying* on us!" Sloan accused.

Zach leaped to Mollie's aid, holding her shoulders down. "Don't move! You may have broken something!"

"Oh-h-h!" Mollie's long groan accompanied her unwilling consent to Zach's decree.

"She was up there spying on us, Zach!" Sloan insisted, pointing to the hole above them.

"I was *not!*" Mollie gritted. "I was punching down hay for the horses. A bee tried to sting me, and I—"

"Shut up, both of you," Zach ordered. "Let's see what's still working."

Between Zach and Mollie, they tried out her arms,

legs, and back. Nothing seemed seriously damaged. Except her pride.

"I'll be fine," she panted as Zach helped her to her feet. "Just let me rest a minute."

Zach turned an oat bucket upside down and helped Mollie creak onto it. She felt like she had hay sticking everywhere.

A small titter emanated from beside her. She looked up, and there stood Sloan, smirking behind her hand.

Mollie burst forth with a stupid question. "What are you laughing at?"

Sloan let out one big guffaw, then another. "It's the Straw Man! From the *Wizard of Oz!*"

Mollie sizzled. But then Zach laughed.

Mollie pulled at the hay sticking out of her hair, her shirt, anywhere it could jam, imagining the clown act she'd just performed. Against her will, she started to giggle.

The barn echoed with peals of laughter. Mollie flopped back into the hay that had mercifully broken her fall, too comic-stricken to sit up. "Oh, baby," she finally gasped, "this has been a day!"

Wiping his eyes, Zach got her back on her feet. "I'll take care of Star after I get you to the house," he promised.

Sloan hesitated a second. "I'll do it," she said.

Mollie marveled. Maybe Uncle Henry had had a sixth sense. Sloan had just committed two acts Mollie would have sworn were foreign to her nature: She'd laughed—the first real, honest laughter anyone at Indian Prairie had raised from her. And she was going to do a tad of physical work—take care of Star. Was there anything the girl wouldn't do to please Zach?

Chapter Nine

A soft, cool breeze moved through the backyard. Mollie lay in the plastic web lounger with Bro the cat at her side, glad to have the hay and dust showered off.

She began to browse through the renovation plans Todd had left for her. A frown creased her brow.

"Some of these ideas would be great," she muttered under her breath, "if we were trying to create a country estate—and money grew on trees . . ."

Zach came out of the house, bearing a covered supper tray.

Mollie sat up straighter to take the tray. "You didn't need to do this," she said. "But thanks."

"I see Wingate's been busy," Zach remarked, nodding toward the papers in her hand.

Mollie handed him the sheaf of plans. He studied them a minute, then let out a low whistle. "The plans are great, but the bottom line'll knock your eyes out."

"My sentiments exactly."

He handed the papers back to her. "I'm no architect, but let me think about this. I'll bet I can come up with a simpler, cheaper way to take out some of the ugly."

"Please—be my guest!"

Zach lifted the towel off the supper tray. "Better eat this before it gets cold."

Mollie eyed a rather strange-looking glop in the middle of her plate. ''Uh, what have we here?''

Zach pulled up a webbed armchair to face her. He grinned. ''That's Sloan's version of shrimp creole.''

Mollie poked at the reddish mixture. ''Sloan cooked this?''

''Yeah. Only she didn't have any shrimp, so she put in a can of tuna. And the instant rice ran short, so she added a few dried beans. She didn't know to cook 'em first.''

Mollie took a tentative bite; she tried to not to wince.

Bro roused himself to sniff at the plate—then leaped off the chair.

Zach said through another grin, ''She's never boiled water before. At least she's trying.''

Mollie put down her fork. ''You've got that right. In every sense of the word.''

Zach picked up a spoon and tasted the so-called shrimp creole. ''Listen,'' he said in a low voice, ''mess up the plate like you've really eaten some, and I'll sneak you a sandwich later.''

''Even a bowl of cornflakes,'' Mollie murmured, surreptitiously scraping part of the concoction into the grass. ''Kitty, kitty, kitty,'' she wheedled softly.

Bro was a no-show.

''By the way,'' Zach said, ''I think I've got the furniture thing worked out.''

Mollie brightened. ''They're going to take it back?''

Zach shifted. ''Well, yes and no. Now, just listen,'' he hurried on as Mollie flared. ''You know the hired man's house? I've put a bug in Sloan's ear. She's always telling me she'd like her own space. She could have it if that house was fixed up. And she could exchange the new lounge furniture for whatever she wants in her own place.''

Mollie leaned forward. ''If Indian Prairie had that kind of money, I'd have guests booked in there!''

Zach put up a hand. ''Indian Prairie won't pay for this. Sloan will.''

''That house hasn't been used for years. When are you going to have time to make it livable?''

Zach laughed. ''I'm not. Ray Jones will know somebody who can do the actual labor. I'll just be the advisor.''

Mollie was silent.

''Think about it. You'd have some space from Sloan. You could use her present room for paying guests. She'd have a project to keep her busy. . . .''

Mollie's slow grin stopped him. ''I think she's already got one. Don't you?''

Zach reddened. ''So you *were* listening in to that little barn scene?''

''Sure,'' Mollie admitted airily. ''And I paid for it, didn't I?''

Zach laughed. ''Dearly. But don't read too much into what went on before you did your skydive. That's just the way Sloan operates.''

''Yeah? You seemed like a pretty willing patient.''

''What did you want me to do? Slap her?''

Mollie's grin turned speculative. ''You're attracted to her, aren't you, Zach?''

''If you mean I notice she's a girl, yeah. I'd have to be dead not to. But lots of girls are . . . girls.''

Mollie shook her head knowingly. ''You're just like all the other men,'' she mocked. ''A pretty face, a cute figure—doesn't take much to get your attention.''

Zach rose, a crooked grin on his face. ''Maybe. But

keeping it's another thing.'' He tweaked her bare big toe. ''Better remember that while you're messing around with Hot Toddy.''

He leaned to pick up her tray. With the delicious aroma of soap, shampoo, clean clothes—and the shining dark hair framing a strong, handsome face—Hot Toddy was far from Mollie's mind.

''Zach.'' She was surprised to find her hand on his muscular forearm, keeping him bent toward her just a second longer. ''Uh, thanks. For last night, and this morning, and—a lot of things.''

She saw fun in his dark eyes—and something more. Attention. Lots of it.

He straightened gradually, looking at her satirically. ''Glad to be of service, m'am. Any time.''

Two weeks later, Mollie watched from the kitchen window as a Quad City furniture truck parked in front of the former hired man's cottage. Two burly men got out to worry a mattress—king size—through the cottage door.

Dee came up from the basement with a basket of clean laundry. She joined Mollie at the window. ''Well, now, that's a pretty big playing field for just one person, isn't it?''

Mollie didn't answer.

''Wonder how much Sloan has spent so far on her private 'studio,' as she now calls it?''

''I don't know; must be plenty,'' Mollie said.

''Refinished floors, rearranged walls, new bathroom fixtures, and—I laugh to mention it—a state-of-the-art minikitchen. What in the hey is *she* going to do with a kitchen?''

Mollie's grin tilted to one side. ''I think she's planning to do considerable entertaining. One guest, only.''

Dee chuffed. ''Zach, you mean? If she's going to cook for him—yuck! That stuff she left in the fridge two Sundays ago ought to be registered as a lethal weapon!''

''Now, now, Dee,'' Mollie said with mock seriousness, ''let's be charitable. You've got to admit, it's a relief to have her wrapped up in her 'studio' instead of bugging us.''

''True. Man! Who but Sloan could afford to pay carpenters double-time to get the place done fast?''

''Not I,'' Mollie said with a sigh. ''Talk about sublime and ridiculous—Sloan's spending a fortune on a three-room getaway. You and I squeezed pennies just to brighten up this kitchen.''

''True. But it does look pretty good, don't you think?''

Mollie glanced around at the freshly painted white cabinets, the cheerful curtains at the windows, the fairly new secondhand stove and refrigerator that replaced the old ones. ''It's not bad. At least the customers shouldn't wonder if they've dropped in on Ma and Pa Kettle.''

''Won't be long now, will it, before customers start coming?''

''Next weekend. A family of three and one of five are coming Friday for seven days. None of them have ever been on a farm before. Should be interesting.''

''One thing, Mol. When Sloan leaves Indian Prairie, you'll have a swell unit to rent out.''

''It looks like she's settling in for the long haul.''

''Oh, she'll leave, Mollie. When Zach does. He's

got most of the repairs made, hasn't he, that he can do with guest around?''

''Well—'' Mollie hesitated.

Dee gave her a long look. ''Just a month ago you hated his guts! Now you don't want him to go?''

''It's nothing personal,'' Mollie insisted. ''But he's come up with some good ideas for making the main house look better without breaking the bank. Things he can do after the summer season. Here, come outside, and I'll show you.''

Dee followed Mollie outside to the front of the house.

''As Todd says, there's no architectural significance to this house. And Lincoln never slept here or anything. So there's no need to preserve for the sake of history. But without major bucks, there's no way to turn this house into a 'statement.' So why not just go for decent? Less offensive?''

''Sounds reasonable to me.'' Dee eyed the homely structure. ''If you can figure a way to do that.''

''Here are Zach's suggestions. First, replace that flat roof on the addition, and that horrible green glass top to the porch, with pitched roofs. Then—'' Mollie pointed to the siding on the addition. ''This yellow vinyl wouldn't look bad if it weren't tacked onto the dirty gray. So if you can't lick 'em, join 'em. Do the rest of the house in yellow vinyl. With dark green trim. What do you think?''

Dee nodded yes. ''I think Zach's got good sense. And I think you'll be real happy to have him stick around longer.'' She whipped back into the house before Mollie could argue.

That evening as Mollie fed the horses, Sloan came strolling into the barn. She eyed the munching herd critically. "Where does one go to pick up a couple of live horses?" she inquired lazily. She had already made known her opinion of the Indian Prairie herd: "Duds! Except for Star—and she's getting old."

Mollie willed herself to maintain her poise. "Well—" She tossed a feed bucket onto its peg. "Depending upon what one wants to pay, one can go—" And she rattled off a list of horse markets with stock ranging from "one step from dogmeat" to "thoroughbreds fit for the queen of England."

"Hmm." Sloan considered. "I think something in the Appaloosa line—and I don't mean that clod, Junior—would suit Zach. Don't you?"

"How do you know Zach wants any kind of horse?"

"He's told me."

Mollie was irked by Sloan's small, self-satisfied smile.

"We've been out riding the last couple of evenings, as I'm sure you've noticed."

Oh, yes, Mollie had noticed. Aunt Gwen had been thrilled when she'd called to inquire "how things are progressing."

"And he's really getting into it," Sloan went on. "He says if he had the money, he'd have his own horse. So—"

A warning signal flashed in Mollie's brain. She faced Sloan, troubled. "Sloan—back off from buying Zach a horse. He won't like it."

Before Sloan could fire off an argument, Zach, followed by Ralphie, who was now out of school and employed full time at the farm, came into the barn. "Zach won't like what?" he inquired.

Neither woman said anything for a second. "An Appaloosa," Sloan finally said, "of your own."

"Sure I would. If I could pay for it."

"How about accepting it for services rendered?" Sloan suggested with a sly grin. "For all the expert advice you've given me about my studio. And *at* my studio."

Zach waved her off. "No horse, Sloan. Besides—" He walked over to a feeding Junior. "If I want to ride an Appie, there's always Dunderhead, here."

Sloan let out a disgusted breath. "*That* boxcar?"

Zach ignored her. "You're not such a bad guy, are you, fellow?" Zach said, scratching Junior's broad forehead.

"Zach—besides being homely, he's *dumb!*" Sloan said.

"So? Nobody's perfect." He rubbed Junior's ear. "You just need love and understanding. And a real good whack on the rear when you get out of line. Like a lot of humans, right?"

Mollie couldn't help laughing at Junior's pricked-ear expression—as if he were thinking, *Now, here's a guy I can relate to.*

"You aren't going to turn that toad into a prince, no matter what you say," Sloan sneered. "And as for riding him—you'd have better luck with a camel!"

Zach turned from Junior. His smile was a bit cocky. "Wanta bet? Fifty smackers says I can ride Junior."

Alarm made Mollie say something she immediately regretted. "Zach, even Todd had trouble controlling Junior—"

A stubborn glint streaked through Zach's eyes. Now his masculinity was challenged.

"I don't want to bet," Sloan said poutily. "It's not worth fifty dollars to see you get hurt."

"No sweat!" Zach scoffed. "I can ride Junior."

Mollie shook her head. Zach was going to prove himself—or die trying.

"Come on, Ralphie," Zach said, "let's finish cleaning up the remodeling debris around the cottage. We'll have the rodeo later."

Sloan watched them walk off. She turned to Mollie. "You're not too smart about men, are you? Zach might have listened to sense if you'd kept quiet about Todd Wingate."

Mollie agreed, but she couldn't bear to let Sloan know that. "I'm a busy person, Sloan. I don't have much time for figuring how to play to the male ego."

Sloan tossed her head. "That's obvious." She stomped off for her studio.

In the early twilight, Zach led a saddled Junior out of the horse barn, into the pasture. Mollie, Ralphie, and Sloan watched from the barn door.

Mollie was worried. She'd been tempted to spirit Junior out of the pasture for parts unknown, rather than let Zach carry out his rash plan. But in the end, she'd decided a man who rode a Harley with reckless abandon could probably survive whatever Junior threw at him.

And Junior threw a lot. Zach might be his buddy when it came to handing out treats, but as he climbed into the saddle, Zach became just another burden to be dislodged.

Junior's performance started with a fast backtracking, followed by a sudden spurt forward. That didn't work. So then he went into the sideways two-step, the quick buck, and the semi-rear.

Zach held on. Mollie admired his grit even as she held her breath for his safety. If he should fall—if Junior should step on him—

"Man! This is all right!" Ralphie observed through an enthusiastic grin. "That dude's tough!"

Whether he meant Zach or Junior, Mollie wasn't sure.

Junior stopped cold. For a second, it looked like he might be going to give up. Zach urged him to go forward, and for a few steps he did—parallel to the side of the barn.

Suddenly Junior lunged sideways; Sloan screamed and Mollie yelled, "Zach, jump off! He'll break your leg."

Too late; Junior was already trotting alongside the barn, rubbing Zach's leg hard against the rough siding.

Just as Mollie rushed to grab the horse's bridle, Zach managed to roll out of the saddle. He hit the ground hard.

"Get over here, you big oaf!" Mollie commanded the snorting Junior, pulling to bring him away from the barn.

Zach let out an expletive. Then he was up off the ground, grabbing the reins and pulling himself up into the saddle.

"Zach! For heaven's sake, get away from him!" Sloan shouted.

"No way!" Zach muttered. "All right, Junior, let's try it again."

Mollie let go of Junior's bridle. Zach's heels nudged him in the belly, and once again he headed for the side of the barn. But this time, Zach was ready with a tremendous whack to the haunch. "Forget it, Junior," he ground out. "You and I are gonna be partners, whether you like it or not."

It took the rock-headed Junior another five minutes to decide Zach meant business. But at the end of that time, he was trotting around the pasture dutifully, if not with enthusiasm.

The spectators finally drew deep breaths. Zach rode Junior into the barn and gave him a measure of oats before he turned him loose for the night.

"I hope you're going to get rid of that menace to society, now that Zach's tamed him," Sloan said to Mollie as the quartet headed toward the house.

"Why?" Zach quizzed, limping beside her. "Junior's my kind of horse—young, spunky, and stupid enough for me to bully."

Even Sloan had to laugh at that.

Later that evening, when everybody else had gone to bed, Mollie noticed a light still on in the kitchen. She went to turn it off. Zach was at the sink getting a glass of water. He glanced at her, a little sheepish.

"Care to join me in a nightcap?" he jested, holding up the aspirin bottle.

Mollie grinned. "What's the matter, got a pain in that 'great natural seat?' "

Zach groaned. "And everywhere else, too." He gulped down the aspirin and water. "Remind me to never join a rodeo."

"Well, you are one heck of a rider, you know," Mollie said. "Not many novices could stay on Junior."

"No, they'd be smart enough not to get on in the first place."

''You sure made an admirer out of Ralphie. And
. . . others, I'm sure.''

''Do you admire me?''

The direct question caught Mollie by surprise.
''Well, sure. I always admire good horsemanship.''

He came closer, studying her eyes. ''That's not
what I asked. Do you admire *me?*''

''Does it matter?''

He set the glass on the table. He came closer still,
so that she felt the warm, young strength radiating
from his body. Slowly, he pulled her into his arms.
''Let's do a test,'' he whispered, ''to see.''

The room swam as he kissed her, gently, thor-
oughly, breaking off only when she finally came to
her senses enough to pull back.

''Zach—we—uh—'' She couldn't think straight
enough to finish.

He laughed softly. ''Back in the old days, when you
were beating me up and putting me down, bet you
never thought you'd have to decide, 'Does Zachary
Kincannon matter to me?' ''

''You did matter, even then. Too much. You were
so mean—I used to lie awake nights trying to think
of a way to get back at you.''

Zach laughed again. His eyes sparkled with
warmth—and mischief. ''If I tell you how to do that,
will you make my life miserable?''

Mollie smiled wryly. ''Depends. What it is that gets
to you?''

''This.'' He pulled her back into his arms, and this
time the kiss was tinged with fire. ''I just hate it when
you make me kiss you.''

Mollie's pulse raced. This wasn't the way it was
supposed to go! He was supposed to be kissing Sloan,

not her! "You nut!" she whispered, trying to laugh over her pounding heart. "Go take a cold shower!"

He held her for one second more, then let her pull free.

"Sure, baby. But don't forget—torture me any time you feel mean."

His soft laughter followed her from the foot of the stairs as she sped up to her room.

Chapter Ten

"Watch it, Ralphie!"

The command emanating from an open upstairs window startled Mollie and Dee, at work enameling the picnic table and some old metal lawn chairs in cheerful greens and yellows.

"Sounds like Zach and Ralphie are having fun installing the air conditioner in your bedroom window," Dee said over a loud pounding.

"I'm not surprised," Mollie said. "That window was stuck tight." She straightened her back, resting a moment from her labors.

"What a stroke of luck," Dee said, "your aunt taking over that rental property with a half-dozen a.c. units stored in a back room. They'll keep the bedrooms bearable until you can afford a new heating and central air system."

"Yes, that was lucky." Secretly Mollie suspected that Aunt Gwen had conveniently "found" those units just to keep Zach at Indian Prairie longer.

Dee chuckled. "Ralphie's never worked a day in his life. I guess you know nobody but Zach would put up with all the boo-boos he's made so far."

"Zach is pretty tolerant of other people's failings, isn't he? Now, if he could just get Ralphie to give up that wild hairdo. And the dangly earring—"

"I know. Ray and I have tried to tell him he'll scare

109

the guests, but you know teenagers and their 'statements'—''

''Look out below!''

Mollie let out a little yip as a heavy object hurtled to the ground not a foot from her.

Zach stuck his head out of the bedroom window. ''That tears it!'' he growled, glaring down at the damaged air conditioner lying on the ground. ''You all right?'' he inquired of Mollie.

She nodded yes.

Zach ducked back through the window. ''I told you to hang on, Ralphie!''

Dee's eyes rolled. ''Oh, oh! Sounds like Little Brother is in real trouble!''

''Not as much as he'd be in if that thing had hit me!'' Mollie gasped. ''Sheesh!''

In a few seconds, Zach stalked out into the yard. He had on cutoffs and a tiny trickle of blood ran down his scraped shin. Sweat gleamed off his bare back and shoulders. He knelt by the fallen air conditioner. ''We can scratch that one,'' he said after a short examination. He rose. ''That was the last unit. I'll put in the one out of my room, Mollie.''

''No, you don't need to do that, Zach—''

''It's okay. I won't be needing it much longer.''

Just then Ralphie slunk out of the house, holding his left earlobe.

Dee gasped. ''Ralphie—your ear! It's all bloody!''

Ralphie flipped back the right-sided hank of hair that was forever falling over his eye. He met Zach's frowning gaze. ''Gee, man—I'm sorry! The air conditioner just slipped right out of my hands!''

''Just slipped when your earring caught on the curtain, right?'' Zach prodded.

"Yeah," Ralphie mumbled.

"So now we've got one dead a.c. unit, and you could run a car axle through that ear if you wanted, right?"

Ralphie flipped his hair again. He didn't answer.

Zach's frown mellowed. "Ralph my man, there's probably a lesson in there somewhere. Go wash off the blood and get yourself a cold drink before we move the unit out of my room."

Dee put down her paintbrush. "I'll go with you, Ralphie. You need some antiseptic on that ear before an infection sets in."

"Zach," Mollie began as soon as Ralphie and Dee disappeared into the house, "what did you mean, you won't be needing the air conditioner much longer?"

"I'm just about finished here, Mollie, with what I can do before the summer season ends."

At least Mollie's first fear was unfounded: He wasn't moving in with Sloan. "But," she said, "I thought you kind of liked it here."

His smile was tired but warm. "Didn't I make that plain the other night? In the kitchen?"

"Oh, that was just . . . messin' around," Mollie said. Nevertheless, her face got pink.

"Whatever it was, I can't stay on Gwen Harris's payroll if I'm not doing anything to earn it."

Mollie's heart did a strange twist. "But Aunt Gwen wants you to stay here!" she blurted. "I mean—" She was flustered.

A cloud passed over Zach's face. "I'm not sure what your aunt wants out of me, Mollie. You got any idea?"

Mollie's conscience tingled. "Didn't you say you owed her a debt?" she hedged.

"Zach! You're hurt!"

For once Mollie was glad to have Sloan burst in between her and Zach. Sloan rushed to kneel by Zach's wounded shin. "Have you had a tetanus shot lately? I've heard about farmyards—I'll take you to the emergency room!"

Zach gave her an incredulous stare. "For cryin' out loud, Sloan, it's just a scrape. The Marines gave me enough tetanus shots to last a lifetime."

Sloan rose, swift as an arrow. She put both hands on Zach's shoulders. "Then stay there. I'll clean up the wound and put a bandage on it." She was off for her studio before Zach could stop her.

Zach jumped to his feet. "This is silly! I don't need a bandage!"

Mollie couldn't stop a grin. "Relax, Zach. She's just a kid, remember? And she *is* trying!"

Thursday: midnight. Within twenty-four hours, the first Indian Prairie customers would arrive.

Mollie stood in the middle of the lounge, surveying the fruits of several visits to the House of Bargains and the decorating efforts of herself and good old Mom. Two club chairs, slipcovered in colorfully striped sailcloth; an oak rocker, refinished by Mom and softened by pads in a flower print that picked up the hues of the slipcovers; a couple of end tables and lamps; and a big rag rug that fit well in front of the fireplace. Mollie nodded affirmatively. Not bad.

Another rug, Navajo in origin and tough as nails, was thrown over some of the flaws in the old leather sofa. A fashionably crummy parson's table stood behind the sofa, supporting a huge bouquet of fresh garden flowers.

Yes. Mollie nodded her head approvingly. It would do.

"Looks real nice. Homey."

She turned, not surprised that Zach was still up. He'd been working late, too, putting the finishing touches on Sloan's cottage so she could move into it in the morning.

"Mom gets a lot of the credit. Dad says she has the nesting instinct."

"I liked your mom, the few minutes I got to talk to her the other day." Zach smiled down at Mollie. "And your dad, too."

"Thanks. I like 'em, too."

Zach moved to the fireplace to examine a large, fan-shaped display of arrowheads hanging above the mantel. "Where did these come from?"

"On loan from Ray. He says his family has been collecting them for years off the land around here. He thought the farm guests might find them interesting."

Zach nodded yes. Then he picked up a small, weathered-wood frame from the mantel. Inside it was a neatly scripted stanza.

"What's this?"

"Oh—well—" Mollie hesitated. Would Zach laugh? "I remembered a poem I read once in high school. By William Cullen Bryant. I . . . thought it belonged here. Sort of in memory of Uncle Henry."

Zach didn't laugh. He read aloud:

> These are the gardens of the Desert, these
> The unshorn fields, boundless and beautiful,
> For which the speech of England has no
>   name—
> The Prairies . . .

He turned to Mollie. "That's really nice, Mollie," he said softly. "I don't know a lot about poetry, but . . . it's just right. Like this room."

Mollie smiled, suddenly shy.

"So," Zach said in a lighter tone, "how do you feel, Ms. Manager, the night before your big enterprise opens?"

Mollie considered. "Glad. But scared. It's just suddenly come pouring over me, how many things could go wrong."

Zach took her by the hand. "Come on," he urged, "let's go outside. I want to show you something."

Mollie went with him, mystified. He took her out to the farmyard, to a spot where, to the north, gentle hills rolled under a full moon as far as the eye could see. Except for an occasional pinprick of light from a farmstead, the whole area looked as it must have far in the past.

Zach pointed upward.

Mollie sucked in her breath. The night sky was blue velvet studded with stars so sparkling they seemed to burn.

"Think how many others have lived here before us, Mollie," Zach mused softly. "How many others have gotten in a sweat about all kinds of stuff. But then they looked up and saw what's awesome—what we didn't create. And we don't have to keep running, except for the little corners we occupy for a few years. So what's to be afraid of?"

"But right now, I don't know whether I can run even my 'little corner.' "

Zach brushed a gentle hand over her hair. "Mollie, you're the toughest little female I've ever met—and I mean that in a complimentary way. You work so hard;

you handle whatever comes your way.'' He laughed, a trifle self-consciously. ''What's that John Wayne line from *True Grit*—'You remind me of me'?''

Mollie's spirits made an upward surge. ''Well, that's just about as good as I can get, isn't it?'' she joked.

''Farm girl—you can do it!''

They stood together a long time, not talking. In the distance, a cow lowed. The faint, earthy aroma of horsehide, the sweet musk of new-mown hay, the flow of air, soft, warm, and tantalizing, over their faces— Mollie loved it. She could have stayed forever beside Zach, lost in the tangy essence—the magic—of midnight on the prairie.

Chapter Eleven

Mollie slid off Star's back. She was in the Outback, on the high-ground spot where Zach had caught up with her and Todd many weeks ago. The Outback was currently reserved for those hard-core believers who liked their camping rugged—tents, no electricity, no running water, no bathrooms except the Porta Potti.

Mollie chuckled as she loosened the saddle girth and took the bit from Star's mouth so she could graze. The hardy campers who'd set up shop here two days ago had struck their tents and headed for the house today. A pack of yipping coyotes scouring through in the night, probably chasing a deer, had scared the be-jabbers out of them.

She looked around. At least the campers had taken their trash with them. Mollie stretched and yawned. Thanks to an impromptu swimming party and picnic at the Shallows, the strip-mine lake best suited to such activity, she had no trail riders to lead. So Mollie had slipped away for the first few minutes of daytime peace and quiet she'd had in two weeks.

Mollie took a blanket roll from behind Star's saddle. She spred it on the ground, then stripped off her outer clothing to the swimsuit underneath. She was no sun freak, but it would be nice to even out the winter white of her legs and back with the light tan of the rest of her skin. She stretched out, tummy-side down, on the blanket. Ahh! The delightful silk of summer air on bare skin!

Mollie rested her head in her hands. Aunt Gwen was arriving later today, and she needed, desperately, this little quiet time to review the past few weeks. And her state of being. To *think.*

The farm had gotten off to a fine start. It had been a good day indeed when Mollie had hired Dee. With her natural efficiency, Dee not only kept the house clean and comfortable and the table supplied with delicious meals, she did it all on a tight budget. When she went home for the weekend, Mollie could be sure the freezer was stocked with plenty of good stuff needing only a zap in the oven or microwave.

Mollie frowned. One thing worried her: Dee was looking a little peaked lately. A little green around the gills. But she pushed off Mollie's inquiries with characteristic sturdiness. "It's just the hot weather," she'd say, or "Riding herd on Ray and Ralphie both is enough to take it out of anyone!"

Mollie smiled. Actually, Ralphie was shaping up. He'd given up earrings for the duration, and after Zach got his hair cut to a cooler, mid-neck length, Ralphie had sacrificed his long lock to the clippers. Now all his head was bald as a cueball, instead of just the left side.

So far, the guests had been easy to get along with— decent people who appreciated the chance to just "chill out" in the country quiet. Parents who wanted their kids to run and play and get acquainted with nature in a relatively safe environment.

She smiled now as she remembered three-year-old James Michael Anthony's first encounter with a horse. His young African-American parents had watched nervously as she'd handed him up for a ride, safe in Zach's arms, on old Pet.

And elderly Mrs. Fiona Duncan, who'd spent a happy week quilting on the front porch while her son and his family rode and swam and fished.

And, of course, Hubert. "U-bear," as he preferred his name pronounced, *and* his ever-ready zydeco accordion.

Mollie snickered aloud. Hubert was retired, a former cook in a nondescript Chicago eatery. He'd spent the first few years of his life in Louisiana. And never recovered. Short, spare, sixtyish Hubert, ever hopeful somebody somewhere would hire him as a club act, could be heard any time of day—and sometimes part of the night—practicing for his big chance. A full week of zydeco got a little wearing; Sloan had threatened to crush his accordion under her Saab. But Zach persuaded her to just go for a long drive—with him, of course—every time Hubert got too much for her.

Mollie stirred restlessly. She should be glad Zach went motoring with Sloan. And ate dinner at Sloan's table several nights a week. Aunt Gwen had certainly been happy to hear it. But . . .

Zach. His image sprang before Mollie's mental eye. Her heart skipped a beat. Mollie laid her head on her flattened hands. She listened to Star cropping grass nearby and the zizz of insects winging around a tuft of wild daisies. Far off, a bird—she didn't know what kind—repeatededly trilled a long, one-note call. Her eyes closed; she drifted in a golden haze and let her thoughts go where they really wanted to be. On Zach.

So much of the success of Indian Prairie Farm was Zach's doing. Not only because of the repairs he'd made. He was also good with people. Especially inner-city people like himself who might feel a little strange their first time in the country.

Plus he'd come up with lots of simple, inexpensive ideas that made the kids love him. One was the varmint-proof ''petting zoo'' he'd fenced in around the old garage. It served as a sort of day care for any baby animals Ray Jones had on hand, such as the current residents, two piglets and a calf just old enough to drink from a bucket.

Was it these extra projects that kept Zach from leaving Indian Prairie? Was it Sloan? Or was it . . . somebody else—like Mollie?

Mollie drove her mind off that possibility. She was supposed to promote a match between Zach and Sloan. If her enthusiasm for the project had paled, at least she hadn't put any roadblocks in the way. Had she?

''. . . Hey? Lady Godiva?''

Mollie jerked out of a mind-numbing snooze. What—who? Her eyes swiveled toward the source of the call; above the foliage of a dense blackberry bush, she recognized Junior's big head. Somebody was on his back, but she couldn't see who.

''Zach?''

''Sorry. Wrong number.'' Todd rode out into view. He sat looking down at her, an ironic smile tilting his lips. ''I'm not the company you were expecting?''

''I wasn't expecting *any* company,'' Mollie said, slipping on her shirt.

Todd laughed, just cool enough to remind her she'd said no when he wanted to hear yes. ''Sorry I interrupted your siesta. Or see-Mollie, as the case may be.''

Mollie stood and stepped into her jeans. ''It would take a lot smaller swimsuit than mine to shock you, wouldn't it, Todd?'' she observed. ''So, what brings you down here in the middle of the week?''

''Business. I have to have an answer on the plans I left you. Is it go? Or no go?''

Mollie hesitated. ''Todd, the plans are wonderful— the brick facade, the new entranceway, the replaced windows. And the second story above the addition— I love it all. But the money for it—it just isn't there.''

''Yes, it is.''

The stubborn certainty of his tone set Mollie's temper on edge. ''Look, we've been through that. The guests we've had so far don't seem to mind Old Ugly. They love the setting. And the horses and fishing. And the three great meals a day. I don't want to take on any debt that would make me hike the rates for a week at Indian Prairie.''

Todd's cool eyes held hers while he ran a hand down the back of his neck. ''Mollie, when are you going to get real? We both know where there's plenty of money to convert that eyesore into something to be proud of.''

''Where?''

''Your aunt.''

''She doesn't own Indian Prairie. She's just overseeing it until Sloan reaches twenty-one.''

Todd snorted. ''You are truly a babe in the woods!'' He dismounted. ''Your aunt's going to have to pay me a hefty consulting fee whether or not you use my plans. Now, why do you think she's willing to do that?''

''Why, the house obviously needs *some* improvement—''

Todd laughed. ''Understatement of the year! Mollie.'' He came closer. ''Do you think I usually take on piddling projects like this?''

Mollie regarded him coolly. "It's my understanding that in the past, Uncle Henry and Aunt Gwen have given you plenty of projects that *weren't* piddling."

"That's true. And this one won't be, either, if you just give me the go-ahead."

"I've told you, Todd—the money isn't there!"

He came face-to-face with her. "Yes, it is. Gwen's up at the house. I've already talked to her, and she's willing to invest."

"You've *what?*"

"When in doubt, go to the real whip hand. The lady with the dough."

Mollie was furious. "You went over my head?"

Todd put both hands on Mollie's shoulders. "Mollie, you've got a lot to learn. Your aunt is looking to get you a fine, prosperous, up-and-coming husband. Right?"

Mollie wanted to shout "No!" But that wouldn't be true.

"Someone like me," Todd went on. "Even if it costs her a a bundle."

Mollie jerked away from him. "Think again!"

"Don't worry," Todd replied confidently. "Gwen's plan for us isn't going to pan out. For one thing, I'm not in the marrying mood."

"Well, goody for you! Neither am I!"

Todd laughed nonchalantly. "So let's get something good out of this for everybody. Give me the go-ahead, and you get a great-looking habitat. I get a healthy fee. Your aunt gets at least *something* to show for her money and efforts. And, uh, by the way, Biker Boy gets to oversee the actual restructuring. Gwen says so."

"Gwen says so?" Mollie had to work hard to maintain control. Never before had Mollie so resented the weight of her aunt's driving determination. She felt used, a puppet.

"Hey," Todd said softly, almost teasing. "Don't get bent out of shape." He chucked her under the chin. "I don't hold it against you that you haven't got sense enough to see what a catch I'd be."

Mollie tried to smile over the turmoil in her heart. At least Todd was openly calculating.

Todd remounted Junior. "Get yourself calmed, honey. I'll see you back at the house." He nudged Junior onto the return trail.

It was a grim Mollie who rode into the Indian Prairie farmyard an hour later. She was prepared to have serious words with her aunt. But a strange sight met her eyes.

Zach, Aunt Gwen, Todd, Sloan, Ralphie, and Dee all stood in a circle around a brown jersey milk cow placidly chewing her cud. Zach had a rope looped around the cow's neck.

"Look what came wandering down the lane a few minutes ago. She must have got loose from the Murphys,' " Dee said, mentioning a nearby dairy farm.

Mollie dismounted. "Has anybody called them?"

"Not yet," Zach said. "The kids are coming back from the swimming party," he went on, motioning toward a group of six youngsters trooping down the lane. "I thought maybe they'd like to see where milk comes from."

"Well, we can't just take a dairy farmer's milk," Mollie protested.

"I'll pay him for it," Zach said. "I'll bet none of these kids have ever seen a cow milked. Come on, farm girl, show 'em how it's done."

Mollie's hands went to her hips. "Me? I've never milked a cow in my life!"

"Huh? Oh, that's right, you dairy at the IGA," Zach joked. "Well, Wingate, how about you?"

"Sorry," Todd said. "My expertise is with horses."

Zach looked around the whole circle. Dee's hands went up in an I-can't-help gesture. Sloan looked as if she thought Zach had gone out of his mind. His gaze stopped at Aunt Gwen.

"Oh, for heaven's sake!" the sophisticated aunt finally exclaimed. "Go get me a good-size bucket, Mollie. And a kerchief for my hair—"

"Aunt Gwen!" Mollie burst out. "You're going to milk that cow?"

"Of course I am," Aunt Gwen said calmly. "As girls, your mother and I milked cows every day. One big reason I couldn't get off the farm fast enough."

With that, Aunt Gwen took the rope from Zach's hands and gave it into Todd's keeping. "Come with me, Zach. You'll have to make me a proper milking stool. And you, young man," she said to Ralphie, "fetch me some twine to tie Bossy's tail to her leg. I don't intend to have her swish it across my eyes and knock out my contacts."

Within a few minutes, Aunt Gwen, kerchief protecting her beautiful hair, sat on the T-shaped stool Zach had just slapped together, her head resting on the cow's flanks. Around her stood six awe-stricken kids— as well as six gawking adults—as she deftly drew a steady stream of warm, foamy milk from a totally unimpressed cow.

Mollie gazed at her aunt in wonder. Here she was, all set to stand up to her aunt for the first time in her life—and here was Aunt Gwen manifesting once again an iron spirit that said, "I can do it, and I *will* do it!"

Chapter Twelve

"Holy mackerel! We've got *how many* coming for the Fourth?"

Dee tapped the notepad lying before her on the picnic table. "One hundred and sixty-four."

"One hundred and—?" Mollie swabbed her beaded forehead. Dee's answer would have made her sweat even if the weather weren't end-of-June, make-the-corn-grow, steaming hot. "When I said, 'Let's have a Fourth of July party and introduce the farm to its neighbors,' I just wanted to show 'em we're no cult. I never dreamed that many people would actually come!"

"It's a good thing Zach has put off going back to Chicago. We'll need all hands."

And it will keep Zach here longer, Mollie thought.

"One hundred and sixty-four people—that's a lot of chicken and pork chops," Dee mused. She turned, stretching out her legs on the picnic table bench. She, like Mollie and everyone else at Indian Prairie, was clad in shorts and the coolest top she could find. She looked tired. "Maybe we should change the menu. Hot dogs are a lot cheaper than chicken or pork chops. And the pies and cakes? The Shawano Kool Treats man has one of those traveling frozen custard do-ma-jiggys. For a crowd like we're expecting, I'll bet he'd be wiling to bring it out here."

"Good. Call the do-ma-jiggy man." Mollie stared at the yellow pad. "You can add one more name to the list. I just talked to Todd Wingate and he's coming down."

"Oh? Feeling better about . . . things down here, is he?"

"He won't give up on the renovation."

Mollie didn't want to talk about the renovation. When she'd finally cornered Aunt Gwen to discuss the subject, her aunt had soothed that, of course, Mollie would have the last word on the project. But Todd *had* mentioned a number of preparations Zach could make before the actual renovation began—projects that could be done with guests in residence. Things that would keep Zach at Indian Prairie . . .

As Mollie had started a heated protest, Aunt Gwen had suddenly noticed the framed Bryant poem on the fireplace mantel. She'd taken it in her hands, then turned to Mollie, tears in her eyes.

" 'These—are the gardens of the Desert—' " she'd read in a hesitant whisper. "Mollie, this is so beautiful. So moving. Did you have these words framed?"

Mollie had nodded yes. "For Uncle Henry."

Aunt Gwen had put the poem back on the mantel, then come to take Mollie in her arms. Gone was all the bravado of the milking episode. All the slyness of the renovation plan. She had laid her head tenderly against Moillie's. "You are so very dear, Mollie. You understand how I feel about Henry, don't you? What would I do without your love? Your support?"

The strong words, the rest of the justified protest—they had died right then on Mollie's lips. . . .

". . . Bodies everywhere," Dee was saying now, "and a mile-long waiting list for reservations. And a

Fourth of July celebration that won't quit—did you ever wonder,'' she queried, waving the notepad under Mollie's nose, ''whether Indian Prairie might turn out to be too successful for its own good?''

Several hours later, Mollie led three kids and two adults out of the woods behind the house. The horses' tails swished steadily against the gnats hanging in lazy swarms in the still-hot air.

''See you all at supper,'' Mollie said after each had dismounted within the horse barn. Ralphie came into the barn to begin the tedious process of unsaddling and feeding each horse.

Mollie started across the farmyard to the house. A sudden, tortured yowl rang out from the barn. ''Ow! Oh—owwww!''

She ran back to the barn. Ralphie, his face contorted in pain, limped toward her. Behind his right foot dragged his damaged shoe, a flip-flop.

''Tony—he stepped on me just now! Oh—owww!'' Ralphie panted.

Mollie knelt swiftly to examine his foot. Across the arch was a swelling purple semicircle; the foot itself was a sick white.

''Oh, honey!'' Mollie murmured sympathetically. ''I've warned you not to go around the horses without sturdy shoes.'' She rose to her feet. ''You sit down over here on the mounting block,'' she said. ''I think your foot's broken. We're going to have to see a doctor.''

Mollie ran to the house. Dee was just putting the finishing touches on a cold supper buffet.

''Oh, my gosh!'' Dee's face went yellowish when she saw her brother's swelling foot.

Zach came along. Within minutes, he had Dee and

Ralphie in the pickup. Mollie watched anxiously as they drove off to an emergency room in the Cities. Then she went in to oversee supper.

It was late when Zach finally came back. Mollie was waiting by the picnic table to hear what had happened.

"You were right," Zach said, getting out of the truck. "Ralphie's got a broken foot, all bandaged up and hurting like the devil. He went home with his mom and dad."

"He'll be laid up for a while, then?"

"Looks like it."

Mollie let out a long, tired sigh. "Well, I guess I'll just have to get up at four in the morning instead of five."

Zach came up beside her. "Unh-unh." His head nodded no.

"It's the only way I can get everything done—" Mollie started to protest.

"You're already doing more than any other two women I know. I'll take care of Ralphie's chores."

"You aren't hired to muck out barns and saddle horses, Zach. I'll find somebody else."

He pulled her gently around so that she was facing him. "Haven't you figured it out yet? I do all kinds of stuff I'm not hired to do."

"Well, yes—"

"Like this." He brushed away the unruly hair spiraling around her cheek and kissed her, softly but confidently.

Mollie had to clench her hands at her sides to keep from throwing her arms around his neck and kissing back. She tried to sound light. "Zach, aren't you getting a little . . . forward?"

His laugh was soft and husky. "I'm gettin' into my

Indian heritage. Kickapoo men liked their women strong and feisty. They also didn't wait to be asked when they thought the ladies needed help.''

Mollie tried to think of some clever comeback; she tried to sort the muddle of emotions—pleasure, anxiety, longing—stopping her tongue. But as they turned to go into the house, she looked up at the night sky. There were the stars, still huge, mysterious, eternal. The same universe Zach had reminded her dwarfed the petty concerns of humans.

And beside her was this man, this vastly helpful, protective, lovable man . . .

For a second Mollie was swept by a sense that she and Zach were part of something. Something very strong. Very right.

Chapter Thirteen

‚‚ W_{ho} the heck is *that*?''

Mollie turned from the kitchen window, puzzled.

Zach rose from the hasty Sunday lunch they'd been taking in the brief period between the departure of the past week's guests and the arrivals of the new. He brushed a napkin across his lips and peered over Mollie's shoulder. ''Well, I'll be a Kickapoo's cousin!''

His comment came as a dusty, well-worn black Chevy pickup, pulling an equally experienced fifth-wheel trailer, bowled into the Indian Prairie farmyard.

''We haven't got trailer park facilities!''

A wry grin creased Zach's face. ''Don't worry. Kish will probably set up a wickiup—a bark lodge—in the backyard.''

''Huh?''

Zach turned to Mollie. ''It's my cousin, James Kishko Kincannon. Professional Indian.''

'' 'Professional Indian'? What are you talking about?''

Zach laughed. ''Kish's got the same amount of Kickapoo blood in him as I have; the difference is, he makes a career of it. Hunts out slights to Native American dignity. And he knows 'em when he sees 'em, because he's an anthropologist-archeologist.''

''That's a mouthful!''

''You bet! And he's a handful. Come on out, Mollie. Meet the distinguished member of the Kincannon tribe.''

Mollie was all curiosity as she and Zach approached the truck. A man with skin like tanned leather was alighting from the truck. His long, dark hair, laced with a few grays, was parted down the middle and tied off behind each ear. He wore jeans, a plain khaki shirt, and an exotically colorful neckerchief. On his feet were deerskin moccasins, obviously handmade.

''Kish, you old dog!'' Zach grinned and slapped his cousin on the shoulder. He introduced the newcomer to Mollie, then inquired, ''What are you doing here?''

Although James Kishko Kincannon appeared to be somewhat older than Zach, there was a definite physical resemblance between the cousins, especially through the eyes. But Kish's dignified stance and the formal cadence of his speech contrasted mightily with Zach's laid-back Chicagoese.

''Cousin, my uncle said you'd come to this place.'' Kish made a long survey of the surroundings, then nodded his head in apparent satisfaction. ''This part of Illinois is the land of our ancestors. I knew you would answer their call someday.''

Zach shifted weight, his grin ironic. ''Actually, Kish, I answered the call of Gwen Harris—Mollie's aunt—to take Dad's place as repairman. Believe me, Gwen is no Kickapoo!''

Kish nodded again, smiling sagely. ''That may be. But you are here.''

With that cryptic statement, Kish turned to the more mundane subject of where to park his mobile home.

''You're planning to stay a while, then?'' Zach asked.

''I'm working on a very important manuscript,

cousin. A dissertation on the aboriginal population of north-central Illinois, circa seventeen to eighteen hundred. I need space. And quiet.''

''Well, uh—'' Mollie stammered. ''You'll need electricity, too, won't you? And water?''

Just then a packed carload pulled in. Doors opened, and kids of all sizes spilled out.

Mollie looked at Zach beseechingly. ''Can you—I mean, I've got to take care of these new guests.''

''Sure, Mollie. We'll figure out something.''

Mollie was busy the rest of the afternoon, but she did have time to worry about the fifth-wheeler now parked under a big tree close to Sloan's house. Mollie could almost promise that Sloan, who'd gone into Chicago for the weekend for a haircut and shopping, wasn't going to like that. After all, her ''studio'' was such a place of private refuge she'd never so much as invited Mollie in to see it. What was she going to think of a scruffy trailer parked right under her nose?

But Zach shrugged off Mollie's foreboding. ''It's the logical place to hook up to facilities,'' he said. ''I'll handle Sloan.''

By eight that night, a backyard circle of young and older guests sat under the stars, listening, mesmerized. It hadn't taken James Kishko Kincannon long to establish himself as this week's star attraction at Indian Prairie.

Kish sat atop the picnic table, cross-legged, back straight as a ramrod, giving forth the history of the Kickapoo.

''I am Kishko, named for a great Kickapoo chief. The Kickapoo were part of the Algonquian Nation. They were a restless people. In fact, the name 'Kickapoo' comes from an Algonquian word, *Kiwigapawa,* which means 'he moves about.' ''

Kish's deep, melodic voice took on an added note of pride. ''The Kickapoo were called 'Lords of the Middle Border.' They moved from the East to Wisconsin, Illinois—including this area right here—and Ohio, as well as south all the way into Mexico.''

''Kickin' the daylights out of other Indian tribes all the way,'' Zach murmured to Mollie. They sat at the far edge of the admiring ring. ''With a Kickapoo in the area, you didn't need the white man to rub you out.''

''Sounds like you've studied up on your Indian background,'' Mollie commented.

Zach chuckled. ''With Kish for a cousin? Are you kidding?''

''The Kickapoo were very successful warriors,'' Kish continued, ''and famed for their independence. In fact, of all Native American tribes, the Kickapoo remnant in Mexico is the only one who never, ever acceded to European rule. But because of their wandering life-style, they did not leave behind a great many artifacts.''

''Have you ever found any Kickapoo arterfacts?'' a small voice asked.

Kish smiled with appropriate gravity. ''Very few. But if I or anyone else *were* to discover the remains of a Kickapoo village or a burial mound, it would be of true historical significance.''

''Like—it would make his day!'' Zach whispered to Mollie.

Kish continued answering questions for the next half-hour. It was getting really dark when the yellow Saab whizzed into the farmyard, shooting gravel as it halted.

Mollie rose. ''Uh-oh! She's back!''

Sloan disengaged from the car. ''Zach,'' she called, ''will you help me unload—''

Sloan stopped dead. She glared through the deepening shadows at the disreputable trailer standing beside her house.

''What is this?'' Sloan's words cut like ice through the gloaming.

The group around Kish stirred restlessly.

Kish, for his part, turned slowly to stare silently at Sloan.

Sloan tossed her head and started toward him.

Oh, boy! Mollie worried. *This isn't going to be pretty.* She thought fast. ''Hey, kids, there are some glass jars on the front porch. Want to hunt fireflies? In the front yard?''

Lithe as a cat, Kish came off the picnic table, rose to his full six feet, and faced Sloan. He strode slowly toward her, stopping about a yard away, viewing her from his lofty dignity.

''Who are you?'' Sloan inquired testily. She flung an arm at the trailer. ''And what is this—this—*thing?''*

Kish's brow went up. ''I am James Kishko Kincannon.'' He nodded toward the fifth-wheeler. ''And *that* is my *home.*''

''Pardon me!'' Sloan huffed. ''But I don't remember giving you squatter's rights next to my studio! Or anywhere else on my property, for that matter.''

Kish's arms folded. ''I don't recall the Sauk and Fox giving the white man permission to steal these, their hunting grounds.''

Zach moved into action. ''Folks—'' He stepped between Kish and Sloan. ''Why don't we get acquainted before you graduate to tomahawks at ten paces? Sloan

Harris, owner of Indian Prairie, this is my cousin, Kish Kincannon.''

Neither party offered to shake hands. If anything, Kish's bearing became even more regal. ''Cousin,'' he said, still focusing on Sloan, ''it is hard to find myself unwelcome on the very land where our ancestors roamed free. Before the European came with his talk of 'ownership' and—'' He made the next word sound like something nasty. '' 'Studios.' ''

In the dim light, Mollie could see Sloan's eyes open wide. ''This is ridiculous!'' the beleaguered heiress cried. ''Zach is no Indian! So how can his cousin be—?''

Kish silenced her with a fiery glare that almost shot sparks. ''Zach does not yet listen to his blood,'' he declared. ''*I* do. *I* am Kickapoo!''

With that melodramatic statement, James Kishko Kincannon strode to his traveling home. The decisive slam of his door left Sloan open-mouthed.

''Well!'' she sniffed finally. ''What do I have to do, call the sheriff to get rid of him?''

Zach tried to play peacemaker. ''Don't get fussed over Kish's talk, Sloan. He's not going to demand a deed to the farm.''

''*He* is not in a position to demand *anything,* Zachary Kincannon. Even if he *is* your cousin!'' Sloan whipped into her studio. The crash of her slammed door echoed across the farmyard.

Mollie turned to Zach. ''Well, street boy, you sure handled Sloan!''

Zach ran a hand over his hair. ''Okay. I struck out for now. Give me time, and I'll get this thing worked out.''

''I hope so.''

Mollie's feelings were mixed. For the first time, Sloan had lashed out at Zach. It wasn't altogether bad that his male ego got a slight dent. But, of course, it wasn't good that Sloan maybe wasn't so taken with him as everybody had suspected. Was it . . . ?

Over their usual early breakfast next morning, Zach asked Mollie to figure out a weekly rent for Kish. "He's no freeloader," Zach said, "and in spite of his plain trappings, he's got a reasonable income. University professorship, book sales—that kind of stuff."

"What about his meals? Will he eat with the other guests?"

Zach laughed. "Kish only eats when he hasn't got anything better to do. Then he might devour a whole cow! Which reminds me, can you spare a couple of ponies so I can take Kish on a tour of the farm later this morning? He knows about the Great Sauk Trail going through here. He'd like to check it out."

"Be my guest! Anything to keep Kish and Sloan apart. Want a picnic lunch to take with you?"

"You bet! Kish may not care about food, but I do!"

Later that day as Mollie headed toward the house after the afternoon trail ride, Sloan intercepted her. "When is Tonto going to get that pile of junk out of my face?" she demanded, pointing to Kish's abode.

"Surely he won't be here long, Sloan. Zach says he's a very busy man."

"I want it *gone! Now!*"

Molly chose her words carefully so as not to rile Sloan any further than necessary. "I-I'll talk to Kish about it—"

"I'll talk to him right now! Where is he?"

"I'm . . . not sure," Mollie half-fibbed.

Sloan marched toward the trailer lounging beneath the tree. She gave the metal door a smart rap.

Mollie watched her, worried. ''I don't think he's in there.''

Sloan tried the door; it was unlocked. Without a word, she opened it and stepped into the trailer.

''Sloan!'' Mollie hurried to the door. ''What are you doing? You can't go in there!''

Sloan turned to her from within the trailer. ''I've already done it.'' She moved further into the room, peering through dim light admitted by half-closed blinds. ''W-e-l-l,'' she drawled, ''this is interesting.''

In spite of herself, Mollie's curiosity drew her into the fifth-wheeler. Surprisingly, the interior, unlike the battered exterior, was in fairly good condition. There was the usual tiny kitchenette, but the living area was actually an office. The dinette table served as desk. On it sat a cell phone, a laptop computer, and a large metal tray screwed into the tabletop. A clutter of miscellaneous items of bone, stone, and hide filled the tray.

Sloan picked up a stone sharpened along one edge and ran it over a finger. ''Must be his hunting knife,'' she scoffed. ''He probably uses it to cut off hunks of buffalo before he eats it. Raw.''

''Sloan, let's get out of here,'' Mollie said. ''We haven't got any right to snoop—''

''What right does this—this Kickapoo kingpin have to blow in here and park on my doorstep?'' Sloan demanded. ''What do you know about him?''

''Well, he's Zach's cousin . . .'' Mollie hedged.

''So what? Let Zach send him on his way.''

''But he's family; you don't just send away family.''

''Don't you?'' Sloan tossed the stone instrument

back onto the tray. "My family never had any trouble doing that."

"What do you mean?"

"I mean I spent a total of maybe, what—three months?—in the company of my father. That's how much he wanted me with him."

Mollie stepped closer. "But that's not true, Sloan! He loved you very much. Didn't he ask you to visit him any time you wanted?"

"Oh, yes," Sloan mocked. "And it was so pleasant. My father trying to fit me in between business deals. Gwen biting her tongue every time he bought me something to make up for the neglect. Such a homey atmosphere!"

"But your grandparents—"

"Have their own lives to lead, thank you very much."

Mollie started to protest. But a thought stopped her: Sloan was probably telling the truth. At least, as she saw it.

"Okay. But Zach's family is different. He's very close to his dad. And, apparently, his cousin."

Sloan frowned and turned away, opening the blinds to let in more light. She began an examination of the high-railed bookshelves lining the living area.

"Hmm. *Archeological Significance of the Prairie du Rocher Experience,*" she read off one book spine.

Mollie's ears pricked up. "Prairie du Rocher? That was a French colony in southern Illinois. My ancestors helped found it—well over two hundred years ago."

Sloan smirked. "My ancestors helped found New England. Nearly *four* hundred years ago." She read off another title. "*Social Anthropology of Mid-American Algonquian Tribes*—" She pulled the book off the shelf and scanned the first few pages. "So—Tonto reads?"

"Tonto writes."

Both women spun at the deep voice emanating from the doorway. Kish, a bright bandanna around his forehead, stepped into the room.

Suddenly the area seemed extremely cramped, what with this very tall, very earthy male presence within it.

Sloan's face reddened. She fumbled in an attempt to put the book back on the shelf, but Kish took it from her. Authoritatively.

"See," he said, running his finger along a paragraph. "Tonto know how to put black letters on white page. Make book." His dark forefinger pointed to the author's name: *James Kishko Kincannon.*

"*You*—wrote *this?*" Sloan's astonishment was clear.

"Ungh!" Kish grunted. "Part of Tonto's doctoral dissertation. Tonto college professor when not taking scalps in cultural wars."

The unmistakable spark of humor in Kish's dark eyes surprised Mollie into a nervous giggle. Sloan, on the other hand, seemed unsure how to respond. "If that's supposed to be a joke, I don't understand—"

Kish's long mouth turned up at one corner in a derisive half-grin. "That doesn't surprise me. Perhaps, after I have showered and eaten, I will explain to you." He turned and pointed to the door. "Now, go!"

Mollie couldn't believe Kish's gall. She watched, transfixed, as Sloan wrestled with her natural inclination to cut down anybody who crossed her, and her obvious fascination with the domineering Kish.

Finally Sloan took a step toward the door. She hesitated, looked up at Kish with a stubborn glint that faded into uncertainty, then departed.

Chapter Fourteen

The sun glinted off two smooth brown backs as Zach and Kish worked into a slightly raised area at the edge of the Outback. Within a grid cordoned off by string, Zach dug. Just outside the grid, Kish gently shook dirt through a rectangular screen mounted on legs. A few feet away, Whip grazed and Junior watched Zach with a bemused expression that said, "What crazy thing is my buddy doing now?"

"Find anything yet?" Mollie asked, riding up on Star.

Kish sat back on his haunches. "A couple of things: A French coin dating from the 1700s. And a broken projectile head, probably a spearhead." He took off his bandanna to mop his steaming face.

"I brought you some lunch," Mollie said, dismounting. "And cold drinks." She took a paper sack and a thermos of iced tea from her saddlebag.

Zach stuck his shovel into the ground. He rubbed the small of his bare back. "And not a minute too soon. Let's get into the shade while we eat."

The three moved some feet to a whispering cotton-wood. While the men quenched their thirsts, Mollie set out food.

"I thought you were going to be busy today helping Dee with last-minute Fourth of July preparations," Zach said.

"I was. But Dee's got some unexpected kitchen aid," Mollie said. "Guess who's back?"

Zach looked his puzzlement.

Mollie faked playing an accordion.

" 'U-bear?' "

"The same. Somebody told him about our big celebration coming up, and he decided to join the festivities."

"Good. I like U-Bear's swamp pop."

Zach and Mollie settled down to enjoy their ham salad sandwiches. Kish, however, ate nothing. He sat by himself, fingering the coin he'd found, and staring off into space.

"Tell me again how you and Kish happened to find the coin and the projectile head," Mollie asked of Zach.

He swallowed his last bite of sandwich. "While we were exploring Indian Prairie yesterday, we stopped here to rest the horses. But Junior—you might know—got his reins tangled in that bramble bush over there. Well, you know old Hambone—he goes into his scared horse act, pulling and pawing away. He worked so hard he pulled that bush partway out of the ground. And there, under it, was charred dirt. Like a fire pit, Kish said—"

Pounding hoofbeats shut off the end of Zach's sentence. Mollie and Zach leaped to their feet just in time to avoid getting run over by Sloan on Shalimar, the palomino mare she'd recently purchased for her own exclusive use.

"For cryin' out loud, Sloan," Zach protested, "what are you trying to do, kill us?"

"Mollie, you've got to get rid of that phony Cajun!'' Sloan demanded. ''If he lets out another one of those stupid bayou screeches—I can't stand it!''

Kish turned to regard Sloan impassively. ''Another one of your ethnic prejudices?''

Sloan rode closer to him. ''Hubert could be straight out of the Boston Blue Book, and his endless practicing would *still* drive me crazy. The same chords, the same yowls over and over!''

Kish stood up, slowly—the picture of the Noble Red man. He took Shalimar by the bridle. ''Your white, Anglo-Saxon ancestors took the same narrow attitude toward those outside of their culture.''

Sloan glared.

Zach stood up. ''Hold it, Kish! Nobody can choose their ancestors. And besides, you and I have got more Scots blood in us than Indian.''

''And I'll have you know—'' Sloan ground out over rage, ''the first member of my family to step on these shores lost his life trying to *buy*—not *steal*—land from your 'morally superior' Algonquians!''

''Was that before, or after, he'd taught the Indian to scalp Frenchmen and steal their furs?''

''He did no such thing!'' Sloan shouted.

Zach stepped between the two. ''Knock it off! Sloan, Kish didn't kill your grandpa. And Kish, Sloan hasn't stolen anything from you. So why can't you just let it go?'' He picked up his shovel. ''If you want my help, Kish, let's stop jawing and start digging.''

Kish held on to Shalimar's bridle a few seconds longer, then turned his back on Sloan and resumed his work.

But she wasn't quite finished with him. ''What are you doing? This is my property, you know!''

Kish's voice was back to reasonable as he answered

without looking at her. "Get down off your very high horse, and perhaps I can explain to you."

Mollie could see a half dozen conflicting replies flick across Sloan's face. But she did dismount. And over the course of the next five minutes, Kish told her of Junior's "discovery," and what it possibly meant.

"The fire pit could be late Sauk or Fox," he explained. "But the French coin we found dates from the late 1700s. That was a period of much trading, and considerable hostage-holding, in the Midwest between the French and the Kickapoo."

"Hostage-holding?" Sloan repeated. "Your wonderful blood brothers were into kidnapping?"

"The French learned the Kickapoo were just as protective of their families as the Europeans," Kish said coolly. "So they got into the habit of capturing Kickapoo women and children and holding them to gain concessions. The Kickapoo then returned the favor. And artifacts got spread around that way."

"So, what is it you expect to find here?" Sloan asked.

"A good question," Kish said, without stopping his work. "Details about Kickapoo village life are rare. French missionaries wrote detailed records of the Native American tribes who would let them in. The Kickapoo didn't."

At least he's an equal-opportunity bigot, Mollie thought after this second blast at the French.

Sloan's lips curled in a near-sneer. "Speaking of writing, I thought you were here to finish one of your learned manuscripts, not play in the dirt."

"I am. I can write all night, when I cannot investigate here." Kish paused, and leveled a gaze at Sloan.

"Since this is your property, and since you evidently have little to do, why don't you help us?"

"You expect me to dig?" Sloan blurted.

Kish walked over to a box under the cottonwood. He picked up a small camera. "I think this would not be too lowly for your aristocratic constitution. At certain points, it is necessary to take snapshots of an archeological dig site. I will tell you when."

Mollie had to turn her head to hide her snicker at Sloan's bewildered, *"What?"*

Mollie began a hurried packing up of the lunch remainders, then mounted Star. She caught Zach's eye. His shoulders lifted in a what-can-you-do? shrug.

On her way back to the house, Mollie reflected on the differences between her and Sloan. If Kish had tried that lordly superiority with her, she'd have told him where to head in. Not that he was anything but gentlemanly with Mollie. But Sloan—spoiled, lazy, self-willed Sloan—seemed as much fascinated with Kish's cool bossiness as she was offended.

Kish *was* physically attractive, fit and taut-bodied, though not so handsome as Zach. Of course, Mollie couldn't think of any other man as handsome as Zach. And Kish was obviously intelligent and well educated. But not quite—what was that Aunt Gwen had said about Zach? Not quite civilized?

Chapter Fifteen

"Woodstock Revisited . . ."

Mollie chuckled in spite of butterflies swarming in her stomach. "Un-unh, Todd. There's no mud and no drugs."

Talk, laughter, the shouts of children frolicking in the Shallows—all mingled above a pulsating boom box and a churning accordion. Underlying that symphony was the rumble of the old tractor Ray was using to pull hayracks full of guests up to the house and barn area for a look-see.

Todd glanced toward the water's edge, where Zach in cutoffs, and Sloan in an amazingly revealing black swimsuit, were serving as lifeguards. "By the way, who's idea was this shindig?"

"Mine. There's been a little suspicion about Indian Prairie amongst the locals. You know—maybe we were one of those off-the-wall groups that sometimes hole up in the country. So I wanted to show our neighbors we're just normal, down-to-earth people. . . ."

Mollie trailed off as Ralphie wandered by, as bald as ever, in ragged shorts held low on his hips by a spiked belt, with a red-white-and-blue sparkly earring and a left-foot cast covered with vibrant graffiti. The boom box on his shoulder blared hip-hop.

Off to one side, Hubert, resplendent in a red satin shirt, black jeans, and bright yellow scarf tied pirate-style over his gray locks, danced as he pumped out Cajun-country music.

''He's our entertainer,'' Mollie said at Todd's satirical look.

Just then Sloan made a lazy plunge into the lake. Todd's grin widened. ''Speaking of entertainment, I don't suppose the locals are used to seeing a centerfold take a dive just any old day.''

His glance followed Sloan as she swam to shore and ambled, dripping, past Kish, who was explaining to some kids the construction of a small wickiup he and Zach had built to shelter ice chests from the sun. As usual, he looked very Native American.

''What were you saying about normal and down-to-earth?''

Mollie shrugged and grinned. ''Okay. But at least we're harmless.'' She resumed stacking paper plates and other picnic necessities on the end of the long table serving as a buffet for the coming meal.

''Why don't you get somebody else to do that so we can talk?'' Todd said. ''I'm not planning to stay long.''

''There isn't anybody else, Todd. We're short-handed to the max.''

''What about Dee? Why is she just sitting in that lounger taking it easy?''

''She's worked like mad on this party. But she's feeling a little under the weather today.''

Zach stopped beside her. ''When do you want me to run the kids out of the water for supper?''

''Any time now, Zach. I see Dad has the big grill ready for the hot dogs, and Mom and Aunt Gwen just went back to the house to get the other food.''

Todd picked a pretzel stick out of a bowl and slowly

bit into it. ''Mollie, when are you going to give me the go-ahead on the house renovation? I mean, I like you a lot, but you've made it plain you're not going to be one of the perks of this small-time job. So I need an answer.''

Just then Sloan handed Zach her beach towel and asked him to dry her back. But not before she checked to make sure Kish was watching.

What was going on here? Mollie knew Sloan had been spending a lot of time at the possible Kickapoo site, escaping Hubert's ever-ready accordion, she said. But was it to be around Zach? Or Kish?

Mollie shook her head. No, Zach said Kish and Sloan dueled constantly over the misdeeds of their ancestors. He was getting sick of it.

''What's that nod mean?'' Todd said now. ''No to my plans? Or to Sloan's flirting?''

''Oh—'' Mollie jerked out of her musings. ''Sorry.''

''Don't worry. Biker-man's only got eyes for you. And I don't blame him. In that dress, you'd make any guy look twice.''

''Oh—thanks,'' Mollie said demurely. Aunt Gwen had brought her the dress, a terra-cotta gauze sundress that floated gracefully around her ankles. ''Todd, I'm sorry, I just can't talk right now. I've got this giant party to keep going. And I don't mind telling you— as we head into supper, I'm nervous!''

Todd let out a bored sigh. ''Go play hostess. I'll find *something* to keep me occupied.''

Todd walked over to Zach; they held a brief conversation, then Todd left the picnic area. Mollie was curious, but for the next two hours, she was too busy to notice whether or not Todd came back.

Meanwhile, with her mother and her aunt taking charge of the food table, and Ray and Zach assisting her dad at the sizzling grill, Mollie circulated amongst the guests, making sure she had a personal word with each one.

At last the sun went down. Zach lighted the huge stack of dead timber he and Ray had hauled out of the woods this morning for a last-minute inspiration—a bonfire.

As a full moon rose over the horizon, the flames leaped high, crackling and sparking in the fresh, soft wind.

The kids, who'd been off in a corner gyrating to Ralphie's hip-hop, came closer to watch a couple of adults move out to Hubert's catchy Cajun beat. Little by little, others came out to dance, a bit self-conscious at first, then two-stepping with gleeful abandon.

Mollie watched from the edges, sipping her one and only beer of the evening. She was tired to the point of exhaustion. Yet she felt tremendous satisfaction that people were having so much fun. And either Hubert was playing much better these days, or she was getting brainwashed by his steady practice. At any rate, the Gypsy flavor of the scene began an excited surge through her veins. Instinctively, she began to dance in place.

''Hey, farm girl—you been at the keg too long? You need a partner for this dance.''

Mollie turned at Zach's jest. His dark eyes glimmered with fun. She matched his grin with a slow one of her own. ''You think you're the only one who can get crazy without any help from booze?''

''Well, let's just see.'' Zach's eyes never left hers while he took the plastic glass from her hand and tossed it into a trash barrel. "Okay, farm girl, show me what you can do."

Zach took Mollie's hand in his and led her into the dance. It didn't matter that neither had ever danced zydeco before. The happy-go-lucky rhythm caught them just like it had caught everybody else. Mollie lost her fatigue in the sheer pleasure of the earthy dance.

Hubert finally brought his current number to a sweeping close; still Mollie stood gazing up into Zach's face.

"Mollie," Zach said finally, "let's shake this place for a while."

"Well, uh—" *What's the matter with me?* Mollie wondered. *Why am I getting all goosebumpy when all I have to do is say no?*

"Come on," he urged, not as a request, but as a soft-spoken command.

Out of the corner of her eye, Mollie saw Aunt Gwen watching her and Zach. Mollie had purposely avoided her aunt all evening. Aunt Gwen's smile was pleasant. But tight.

Mollie hesitated a moment longer; then she laughed, trying to make light of Zach's request. "What is it you've really got in mind?"

He smiled, his eyes searching deep into hers. "Somethin' disgusting, despicable, and kind of immoral."

It was a joke, but it caught Mollie off-guard. "Clue me," she said uncertainly.

"Follow me." He guided her out to the road leading into the Shallows area, then to the end of the line of cars parked alongside. The very last vehicle in the line was the Harley.

"How—how did this get out here?" Mollie stammered.

"Todd took it for a ride. I told him to park it here."

"Oh. Well—"

Zach pulled two helmets off the handlebars. He handed one to Mollie. "Are you willing?"

Mollie knew she should say no. But why was her breath shutting off?

Gently, Zach placed a helmet on her head. Then he mounted the Harley. "Come on, baby." He motioned for Mollie to get on behind him.

Mollie hesitated; but she could no more refuse than fly. Gingerly, she mounted the passenger seat. Had she taken leave of her senses?

Zach kicked the Harley into life. "Hang on," he warned needlessly.

Mollie's grip clutched his waist. He started out very slowly, gliding as quietly as the Harley would glide toward the main road. Once there, he stopped. "Okay, honey—hold on tight."

Suddenly the Harley gunned from zero to—? Whatever it was, it took Mollie's breath away. They flew down the road, hair batting madly at the rims of their helmets. At first Mollie was scared. Her arms slid all the way around Zach's hard-muscled waist and she clung against his back like a burr.

But as they rode, a sweet, wild freedom new to her swept her senses. She loosened up and let the wind wash her face like a mad geyser. She couldn't think; she could only feel—light, young, free!

In what seemed too short a time, Zach slowed the bike until he could make a swooping U-turn. He headed back toward Indian Prairie, but instead of turning down the road to the lake, he turned sooner, motoring into woods dark except for the headlight.

Mollie wondered where they were going. She could

tell they were following a cow path, and climbing. But she didn't care. She was with Zach. That was all that mattered.

The cycle stopped. There was a moment of silence broken only by the faraway din of the lake party.

Then: "You can let go now."

Mollie's arms unwound from Zach's waist. He held the cycle steady while she dismounted, then set the kickstand and got on his own two feet. They stood very close together. He took off his helmet, then hers.

It happened, just like in the movies. Slow motion. She was in his arms; his lips were claiming hers; she was drowning in a silky pool of luscious sensations.

"Mollie!" he whispered at last, burying his face in her rich, soft hair. "Mollie, this is what I've wanted from the first day I saw you out here."

It was all she could do to collect her wits. "Zach—where? Where are we?"

He turned her so that together they could look out over the prairie rolling to the horizon. "Remember? The highest point on the property?" Zach turned her back into his embrace. Through half-closed eyes, she could see his smile before he kissed her again.

"That day I came out here—I knew this was where I'd really kiss you for the first time."

Mollie jolted in his arms. "What? Who said—?"

"Shut up," he murmured tenderly. His lips found hers again, and she melted against his steely frame.

"Zach." She was finally able to speak, but she couldn't let go of him. She tried to rise above the longing for him clamoring for satisfaction. "This—can't be. Not now. Not ever."

He pulled away so that he could stare down into her eyes. "Why not? You know we should be together."

"No, we can't—"

He tipped her face up to his. "What's to stop us?"

She stepped back a bit, trying to regain perspective. "Well, for one thing . . ." She was grasping for a straw—anything to give her a chance to clear her head. "For one thing—Sloan."

"Sloan? What's she got to do with this?"

"Zach, you know she's . . . interested in you," Mollie stammered.

"But I'm not interested in her. Not that way."

"Not even a little attracted?"

Zach hesitated. "No. Well—" His shoulders lifted. "Sure, it was kind of a temptation at first to do a little fooling around. But that's not the way I operate. Mollie, you must know that."

Mollie squirmed. "But maybe you *could* like—love—her?"

Zach frowned. "Sloan's looking for a man to lead her around. Somebody to tell her 'Do this, and don't do that'—the way her father should have." He shook his head. "I want to be 'daddy' to my kids, not my wife!"

He drew Mollie back into his arms. She lay her face on his broad chest, hypnotized by his steady heartbeat.

"I'm not offering you a one-night stand, Mollie," Zach whispered softly. "I'm talking marriage, family, mortgage payments—the whole bit!"

"But Zach—you like your freedom. The excitement of city life—"

"I love this place! I didn't expect to, any more than I expected to fall in love with you. But it's happened. I know what I want, and *who* I want."

"Zach." Mollie pulled back, trying to speak over the pain in her heart. "You've changed your mind so fast—how do I know you'll feel the same way five years from now? A year from now?''

Zach turned Mollie's face up to his. The moon gilded his shining black hair, his dark, warm eyes. ''You love me, don't you, Mollie?''

Mollie wanted to deny it; she wanted to extract herself from his loving embrace. But she was paralyzed by truth.

''Yes.''

''And I love you; I'd give my life for you. I'll never change my mind about that.''

Mollie's brain reeled. She saw the disaster for Indian Prairie if Sloan found out Zach preferred Mollie to her. She saw the sadness in Aunt Gwen's blue eyes, felt her dismay over the smashing of Henry's dream.

But Mollie loved Zach. There wasn't a doubt in her heart: She loved Zach.

Mollie managed to pull free, walk a pace away from the man she loved. ''Zach.'' she whispered, her back to him. ''Could we take it slower? We've only been together here at Indian Prairie, what—two months? Could we give ourselves more time to be sure?''

There was a silence. Mollie could tell Zach was fighting his desire to overwhelm her verbal defenses— which he might well do if he persisted. . . .

''Well, if it means that much to you, Mollie.'' She heard struggle in his voice. ''I thought we were on the same wavelength. I'm sorry. I didn't mean to come on too strong.''

''No!'' The denial burst out of her. ''No—you haven't done anything wrong. I—we—just need time. . . .''

Zach came to her, put his arm around her shoulder,

and tipped her face up to his. ''Mollie, I would never push you into anything you weren't ready for.''

Oh, but you have, Zach! Mollie's heart cried. *You're everything I've ever wanted in a man, and you've made me love you. I wasn't ready for that.*

''Whatever time it takes . . .'' He kissed her tenderly, then led her back to the motorcycle. ''We'd better get out of here before I forget what I just said.''

Mollie tried to smile. But inside, her heart berated her: *Liar! Creep!*

Chapter Sixteen

"Well, Mollie—the silence is deafening."

Mollie looked up from the rim of her coffee cup into her aunt's grim blue eyes. She was exhausted from no sleep; her eyes stung with held-back tears; she was fighting to keep control of her tumultuous emotions. "What is it you want me to say?" she asked finally.

Aunt Gwen rose from her untouched breakfast. "How about an explanation. For running off with Zach last night—leaving your parents and me to make excuses and close out the party? For riding back at midnight on that motorcycle? For strolling across the farmyard with Zach, so close you two looked like one person with four legs!"

"You were watching?" Mollie accused.

"Of course," Aunt Gwen replied, unabashed. "And no doubt Sloan was, too, from her studio. What a time to indulge in a spur-of-the-moment tryst!"

"It was no tryst!" Mollie denied, sickened by such a cheap description of what had taken place last night between her and Zach.

"Shh! Don't waken the guests." Aunt Gwen put a hand on Mollie's shoulder. She looked long into her niece's eyes, fatigue, concern, kindness showing in her own. "Mollie, this is exactly what I feared when I made you manager of Indian Prairie. I don't judge

154

you. You think I've forgotten the fires of early youth? A vastly attractive man like Zach, a beautiful night— it's easy to lose your perspective. I understand.''

Mollie rose quickly. ''No! You don't! Aunt Gwen, Zach and I care for each other! He wants to marry me!''

For a second, Aunt Gwen stood speechless. Then she sank onto a kitchen chair. ''Mollie, Mollie, Mollie. All I've tried to do for you—and Zach. Advice, jobs, chances to marry the right people—I hope you noticed Todd Wingate left this morning without saying good-bye to you. All my efforts . . . up in smoke!''

''But Zach doesn't love Sloan. He never will.''

''Mollie, you led me to believe they were getting close. You said they spent a lot of time together; ate meals together—''

''They did. But it was just . . . friendship. On Zach's part, anyway.''

Aunt Gwen regarded Mollie through tear-filled eyes. ''The best relationships begin with friendship. That's how Henry and I started.''

Mollie felt terrible—guilty and confused and . . . re-bellious. ''But they have to go on to something more,'' she argued. ''They don't just stall on friendship.''

''Given time, perhaps Zach and Sloan *would* have gone on to something more, if you'd kept yourself out of the way.''

Aunt Gwen's words stung like nettles. ''I did not mean for this to happen,'' Mollie insisted.

''Henry's last wishes—that Indian Prairie flourish, that Zach marry Sloan—what more can I do to carry them out? I've got the two together; I've promised Todd a great deal of my own money for house renovation, just to *keep* Zach here. And I thought I had your promise to help—''

''So that's what this is all about!''

Both women startled at the sound of Zach's voice. He stood in the doorway to the dining room, slapping an envelope against his palm, his eyes black, his face unreadable.

Mollie was too stunned to speak.

''This little note Wingate left outside my door.'' He held up the envelope. '' 'Could you please get Mollie to agree to my plans for renovating the house? It'll mean a long job and a hefty paycheck for you if she says yes.' ''

Zach came into the room. ''Thanks, ladies, for clearing that up.''

''Zach,'' Aunt Gwen began, ''don't misinterpret—''

Zach's short laugh was rough. ''I don't think I'm misinterpreting anything. I think you're feeling guilty for all the ways you've let Henry down, and now you're willing to sacrifice Sloan, Mollie, me—whoever it takes—so you can feel better. Well, count me out!''

''How have I let Henry down?'' Aunt Gwen bristled.

Zach emitted another harsh chuckle. ''Well, for starters, how about the ways you kept Sloan out of Chicago? Like the time you insisted Dad tear up the guest room, just days before she was to come for the whole summer?''

''I had that remodeling planned long before Sloan agreed to visit!''

''Then there was that mysterious fever you got just when Henry found time to take her on a camping trip. Just the two of them.''

''I don't recall discussing any of those events with you, young man!'' Aunt Gwen huffed.

''You didn't. You thought I was just a bothersome kid hanging around with my dad. But I couldn't help pickin' up on your true feelings for Sloan—'Keep out of my face.' ''

''She was so exasperating! You didn't know her then!''

''True. But I know my dad. And you weren't above using his drinking problem, which he'll deal with the rest of his life, to force me into your service. You didn't mind tearing up his pride—and my life.''

Aunt Gwen gasped.

''Please don't fight!'' Mollie begged.

''I've had my say,'' Zach said, too quietly. ''But I'd like a word with you alone before I put this place way behind me.''

Aunt Gwen stepped aside. ''I won't be in your way. I'm going back to Chicago, Mollie. To celebrate the end of Indian Prairie. Of Henry's dream.'' She fled the room in tears.

''Zach,'' Mollie pleaded, coming close to put her hand on his arm. ''Please—listen to me!''

Zach removed her hand. She had never seen his face so cold, so unforgiving. ''You lied to me. You used me. You put your aunt's big plans ahead of everything else.''

''Zach, that's not true. Aunt Gwen and I thought we were giving you a chance to marry someone beautiful and wealthy—someone who adores you—''

''Hey—I'm a big boy, I can handle whatever comes down the pike. But Sloan's a kid. Did you ever think what you might be doing to her?''

"We honestly thought you'd be good for each other."

"Ha! Nobody has ever worried that much about what's good for Sloan. Just what would salve their conscience. And now you've helped her get all wrapped up with one more person who doesn't love her enough?"

Mollie couldn't get words out. Her tongue was tied with guilt and shame. "I-I didn't mean for her to get hurt—"

Zach's eyes pierced into hers. "I can believe Gwen Harris could play with people's hearts. But you, Mollie?" He shook his head slowly, a pained frown creasing his brow. "I really believed you were the best, the truest, person I'd ever known."

The words were an arrow to Mollie's heart.

Zach pushed past her and strode out the door.

"Zach! Wait!" Mollie cried, running after him as he headed for the horse barn.

Dee drove in; she slammed on the brakes as first Zach dodged her car, then Mollie.

"What are you going to do?" Mollie demanded as Zach stayed ahead of her.

He entered the barn and began measuring feed. "I'm gonna do the morning chores." He turned to face her, fierce as an eagle. "What did you think, I'd walk out before you could get somebody to take my place? When I say something, I mean it."

"Zach, *please!* Let me explain—"

"Oh, yeah! You're real good at explanations." He returned to mixing feed. "But I don't want to hear 'em."

For a second she could hardly breathe. Then anger

mixed with her pain. The strain of the past months, the divided loyalties . . .

"Oh, you're so big-minded!" she jeered. "Where's all the understanding, all the forgiveness you had for Sloan's mess-ups? What am I, dogmeat?"

He turned to her slowly. She would never forget the hurt, the distrust in the dark pools of his eyes. "You're the woman I love. And you took my love and trashed it."

Mollie's turmoil boiled over. She clenched her fists in frustration. "Get out!"

"I'll stay till—"

"G-e-t o-u-t!" she ground through tight teeth. "I won't live with your holier-than-thou attitude! The best thing you can do is get out!"

There was an instant of dead silence. Mollie felt the very ground giving way beneath her feet. Zach looked white under his tan. But neither proud character could bend.

Without another word, Zach dropped the feed bucket and strode past her. She stood trembling with anguished rage, too shocked even to cry. Presently she heard the Harley roar awake, then barrel down the drive. A few minutes later, Aunt Gwen's Mercedes glided out.

Like a zombie, Mollie went through the motions of feeding and grooming the horses. A little girl ran into the barn, wanting to get an early start on a trail ride.

"Sure, honey," Mollie said to six-year-old Tessa, who, if she could have her way, would spend the entire day riding or touching or just looking at good old Pet. "We'll go out in a few minutes. Let's go up to the house and tell your mom where you are."

Across the farmyard, up to the house, making conversation she couldn't remember a second later, Mollie and Tessa reached the kitchen door. Mollie opened it—and let out a suppressed yelp.

"Dee! What's the matter? Tessa, get your mom!"

Crumpled on the kitchen floor, Dee lay still and pale. Unconscious.

Chapter Seventeen

Mollie searched Ray Jones's plain, honest face as he came out to her in the hospital waiting room. He smiled, but she saw a hint of anxiety.

"Dee?" she inquired, standing quickly.

"She's going to be fine—I think. Dee is pregnant."

"Oh, Ray, I've been wondering! Is . . . is the baby all right?"

Ray patted her hand. "Sonogram says so. But, Mollie, the doctor says Dee will have to stay off her feet for at least the next six weeks."

"Why didn't she tell me?"

"I've wanted her to. But you know Dee—she's worried about letting you down. Says you've already got enough problems—"

"I haven't got any problem," Mollie interrupted firmly, "worth jeopardizing this pregnancy for. And that's just what I'm going to tell Miss Dee. Can I see her now?"

"Sure. We can take her home with us." Ray gave Mollie's hand a squeeze. "I know you'll say the right things to Dee, Mollie. Set her mind at ease."

And Mollie did. By the time she and Ray helped Dee into her own home, Dee was feeling much better. Mollie, on the other hand, was hoping against hope no other shoe dropped before Dee was back on her feet again.

The next week passed uneventfully, except for work—dawn-to-midnight, unending work. Mom— good old Mom—baked and roasted and froze main dishes and desserts to fill the Indian Prairie freezer, so that Mollie, between trail rides and chores, could rush in and feed her guests.

Mollie had an ad running for help—kitchen, horse care, yardwork—any of the multiple duties once held by Zach, Dee, or Ralphie, but so far nobody had applied.

Even in the midst of unrelenting labor, Mollie grieved, and raged, over broken ties with Zach, and with her aunt. She'd tried to do something good. How could they be so cold?

Kish took his cousin's disappearance matter-of-factly. After all, Zach was a Kickapoo, a wanderer.

Sloan was a different story. To Mollie's surprise, she didn't say anything, not a word, about the sudden departure of her unliked stepmother or her very-much-liked Zach. But she watched Mollie. Time after time, Mollie looked up to find Sloan regarding her with something in her eyes—definitely not friendship—that Mollie couldn't quite define. It made Mollie uneasy. If only Sloan would be her usual self and attack with nasty innuendo, maybe Mollie could vent some of her inner turmoil.

And then the real heat set in. Torrid, rainless, July heat that dried the grass to straw, the flowers to wilted stragglers. The petting zoo animals consumed water at a rate that kept Mollie hopping. Trail rides had to be postponed until nearly dark, lest the sun fry the participants. Flies bit; fish didn't; air conditioners roared; tempers frayed.

Day after day—heat, work, stress. Was there ever a

time, Mollie wondered, when she'd had more than five minutes just to breathe?

July steamed on; August came. And so did disaster.

Mollie wakened one morning at her usual hour, four o'clock. She was bathed in sweat; her room was strangely quiet. The air conditioner's usual clamor was quieted.

Mollie climbed out of bed, pushing her wet mop of hair off her forehead. She felt sticky all over. Then she realized she hadn't wakened to her clock radio; it wasn't running, either.

"Oh, no-o-o!" Mollie whispered. "The electricity is off. I wonder how long?"

She clambered into clothes and hurried downstairs. By light of the kitchen window, she found the phone number for the power company.

The canned message on the other end of the line was grim: The whole area power grid was down, drained by the massive heat wave. Mollie listened in panic. There was no prospect of restoring power to rural areas for days, perhaps longer.

The whole farm operated by electricity! There would be no lights, stove, refrigerator, freezer, water pumps—not even a fan to blow the hot air around, let alone an air conditioner to cool it!

Mollie staggered to the freezer to check its contents. So far, so good, but that wouldn't last long. She pulled back her hair and stood thinking: There was nothing to do but send the guests home with a refund, and cancel next week's newcomers. On one level, Mollie deducted the lost revenue from her already strained budget. On another, she fought the desire to pack her bags and run, whimpering, to Mom and Dad for sanctuary.

The kitchen door slammed, breaking into her reverie. "What's going on here?" Sloan demanded. "My air conditioner's off—and I can't even get a drink of water!"

"Of course not," Mollie said. "There's no electricity to run the water pumps."

Sloan's brows shot sky-high. "No elec—you didn't pay the bill?"

Mollie gritted her teeth. Why did Sloan have to pick this moment to return to nasty? "Sloan," she said, dangerously calm, "the whole power grid for this area is down. There's no juice for miles around."

Sloan stood frowning in her carelessly thrown on shirt-over-pajamas. Her hair spiked comically over her left ear. "But—I've got to start the day without a shower? I can't even brush my teeth?"

"Of course you can."

Sloan whipped around to face Kish standing in the doorway. "You can bring water from the strip mine lakes—"

"Ugh! Dirty water?"

Kish viewed Sloan pityingly. "Boil it, if you're afraid to drink it. As for me, I'm going right now to bathe in the Shallows—as I do every morning. It is the Kickapoo way."

Sloan stared at him. "Isn't it cold this time of day?"

"Invigorating. Come along if you wish." A wry smile twisted his lips at Sloan's increased frown. "I know how modest you are, so don't worry, I won't look at you."

"Well," Sloan muttered after a moment, "I can't stand to look—or feel—like *this!*" She followed Kish out the door.

Mollie was glad to be rid of the skirmishing pair.

She had plenty to bother her without their bickering. The first chore would be to bring lake water to the bathrooms so that guests could at least wash their hands. She found an empty barrel in the toolshed and loaded it into the back of the pickup.

At the Shallows, Kish helped Mollie fill the barrel. Back at the house, she lugged several pails of water to each bathroom.

By ten o'clock, she had all the guests refunded and shooed off for home. This afternoon, she would have to get on the phone and cancel next week's group. In the meantime, she trudged out to the horse barn to begin her belated chores.

Sweat poured off Mollie as she fed the horses and groomed their hooves. She let them back out into their pasture and started mucking out the stalls. Ray would be here soon to drive away the "honey wagon." She hoped.

As she worked, Mollie remembered Zach—the way he'd done these chores so she could go on her date with Todd. The way he'd taken them over after Ralphie got hurt. With the endless ache that never went away, she remembered how much he'd done to make the farm a success. How much she loved him. How little he deserved her anger.

By noon the petting zoo animals were out of water again. Once they were cared for, Mollie went into the house and began making cancellation calls.

For hours, Mollie had seen nothing of Sloan or Kish, which wasn't all that surprising, since each was a creature of lone habits. She had eaten nothing, but sometime or other, Kish had brought to the kitchen a bucket of lake water he'd boiled over an open fire, so at least she could quench her thirst.

By time the cancellations were completed, Mollie had to return to animal care. The sun was hanging low when she finally finished and started for the house.

Sloan came out of her studio and slung a couple of suitcases into the Saab.

"You're leaving?" Mollie asked.

"I'm going to get a motel room in the Quad Cities. I heard on the car radio they have power restored."

Mollie was so hot, tired, and empty of energy she could only nod.

"Well, what are you going to do?" Sloan asked grumpily. "Sit around and wait for civilization to reappear?"

"Sit around?" Mollie roused long enough to stare at Sloan. "Sloan, the animals have to be fed and cared for—including your Shalimar—whether or not we have electricity. The phone has to be answered. The house has to be looked after. I haven't sat down all day!"

"You mean—" The speculative gaze returned to Sloan's eyes. "The girl who can do anything, who can think—and plan—for everybody else, finally has more than she can handle?"

"What are you talking about?"

Sloan leaned against her car; her smile would have been gloaty—except for the faintest sad twitch at one corner. "All my life, I've been hearing about Mollie Moreau, the Wonder Girl. 'Mollie's so bright; Mollie's so dependable; Mollie's so on top of everything'— from Gwen, from my father. And from Zach."

She turned away for a second, but Mollie caught a glint of tears in her angry eyes. "But Zach found out about you, didn't he? How you're just like your dear, calculating Aunt Gwen?"

Mollie's breath stopped. "He told you?"

Sloan faced her squarely. "When I saw Zach getting ready to leave that morning, I ran after him. I begged him to stay—or to take me with him. So he told me the truth about why he was leaving." Sloan's voice rose higher. "He didn't want me to think it was anything I did. He wanted me to know that he liked me. That he *cared* what happened to me!"

"But Sloan, lots of people care about you. Your father—"

"Ha!"

"Sloan." Mollie tried to find the right words. "The whole plan to get you and Zach together—your father loved you so much. He wanted you to find something good in Indian Prairie Farm. He wanted you to have the best possible husband—"

"A bit late for him to start worrying about little Sloan, don't you think? And what was the rest of your plan? Marry me off to Zach so you'd keep your 'dream job,' and still play around with Zach on the side?"

"No!" Mollie shook her head, frowning, trying to explain. "I went along because I love my aunt, who's been as good to me as—she *hasn't* been to you. And she wanted to carry out your father's plan because she loved him. Just plain loved him."

Mollie's shoulders went up in her effort to get through to Sloan, who only stared. "Don't you see, Sloan? Everything that's been done—no matter how far it's gone wrong—has been done out of love."

"Really? I haven't had much experience with that emotion."

"Not even for Zach?"

Sloan shrugged. "I knew all along he would pick

you. You always win. But—he liked me. He was the best friend I ever had.''

''Sloan.'' It was hard to get the words out, but they had to be said. And Mollie meant them. ''I am sorry to the bottom of my heart for interfering in your life. I had no right; it was completely wrong. If it's any satisfaction, I'm paying a terrible price: I've made a mess of Indian Prairie Farm, and—I've lost Zach.''

''You care that much for him?''

Mollie looked away. She thought her heart would break. ''Only as much as life itself.''

She started for the house. Just as she reached the back door, the whole, dreadful weight of the past few weeks swooped down on her, shattering her control. She stumbled on the stairstep. Suddenly she melted onto the step, resting her head on her arms as a torrent of pain and regret washed out through her tears.

It was some time before Mollie's sobs quieted and she became aware that someone was standing in front of her. She lifted her head, wiping at her eyes with hands grimy from work.

''Until the electricity comes back on, I could help you with the work.''

It was Sloan. Her tone was sulky—but it was an offer of help!

''I can't leave Shalimar here to fend for herself, so I might as well take care of the other horses,'' she said, not meeting Mollie's bleary eyes. ''Unless you'd rather I cooked.''

''Uh, no! The horses—I'd really appreciate that,'' Mollie stammered.

Kish was coming toward them through the near-darkness. ''If you are hungry, I will fix you a meal. I'm used to making do with whatever is at hand.''

"Why, yes." Mollie got to her feet, struggling to find a tissue in her shorts pocket. "Dee always keeps plenty of canned goods. And there's some meat in the fridge that won't last another day—"

"I'll call you when the meal is ready," Kish said, moving past them and into the house. "In the meantime, please find more fuel for the fire."

"Sure." Mollie started for the nearby woods, still unbelieving that help—albeit dicey—was at hand.

Midnight: Mollie and Sloan lay in webbed loungers, Kish on a sleeping bag right on the ground. Anything to catch a breeze in the breathless night.

Kish's meal had consisted of ground meat boiled over an open fire with handfuls of cornmeal and a smidgen of salt thrown in. A strange concoction—Kickapoo, no doubt—but after Mollie's day, she'd have eaten Junior if someone had barbecued him. Even Sloan had tried a few bites, but she soon turned to a can of cold green beans for sustenance.

As Mollie lay waiting for merciful sleep, she pondered. In her wildest dreams, she'd never imagined Sloan was jealous of her. Mollie Moreau, Wonder Girl? The girl who could do everything, win everything? That would be laughable, if she didn't feel too bad to laugh. On the other hand, she'd always seen Sloan as the girl who got all things her way.

How amazing it was, the skewed perceptions people could have of one another . . . Of what was right . . . Of what was love. . . .

Chapter Eighteen

It was five days before electrical power was restored to Indian Prairie. During that time, Sloan did a good job caring for the horses. She took the sudden fall from luxury studio to campfire food and backyard bed better than Mollie expected.

On the other hand, the primitive life was no novelty to Kish. Besides "being Kickapoo," he had spent much of his adult life in rugged archeological camps all over the Americas. He thought the practical solution to water and bathroom problems was for the three residents at Indian Prairie to pitch camp at the Outback lakeside facilities.

The suggestion met resounding defeat. Mollie expected him to go his proud way alone, especially since he was already spending as much time as possible at his dig site. Then she observed a surprising scene: Sloan was lugging a pail of water from the pickup bed to the tripod Kish had set up for boiling purposes. Kish came out of his fifth-wheeler, watched Sloan for a second, then strode to her side.

Masterfully, but gently, he took the bucket from her hands. "This is too heavy for you."

Sloan's eyes fluttered; over a soft blush, she murmured a hesitant "Thank you."

From that time on, Kish became the household water supplier—and a welcome conversational buffer between Mollie and Sloan in the long evenings after supper. Instead of struggling to talk to each other, they focused on Kish, his adventurous digs into past Native American history, and fervent excursions into present-day Indian causes. He was a willing and often dryly humorous lecturer. One evening after Mollie's eyes had begun to droop and she'd retire to her lawn-chair bed, Sloan began quizzing Kish about the dig on her property.

"I still think it's a bit nervy, the way you started this project without so much as a by-your-leave from me," she stated with a half-serious pout.

Out of the corner of her eye, Mollie saw Kish's confident smile. "The honor of starting this project goes to a horse of Native American breed. Junior. It was an act of fate."

"Fate? Does fate know about property rights?"

Kish's smile remained. "Did you know, dear one—"

Dear one? Mollie's ears pricked.

"That the state of Illinois steps in to protect possible Native American burial sites?" Kish continued.

"But you don't know that anybody's buried in the Outback," Sloan protested.

"Not at this point. But since the only other major Kickapoo site in Illinois is the Grand Kickapoo Village discovered near Bloomington, Illinois, the Illinois Historic Preservation Agency would take great interest in any further discoveries."

"But it's *my* land—"

Mollie was struck by the softness of Sloan's protest—almost as if she enjoyed being contradicted.

The answer was equally mild. "It was the Kickapoo's—and the Sauk, Fox, Potawatomies, many tribes'—first.''

Why does this sound almost like—acting? Mollie pondered before sleep carried her away. *Maybe because they're no longer really mad at each other . . . ?*

On Friday, Ray found a neighbor boy willing to take on Ralphie's horse duties until school started. A relieved Mollie called on the Joneses to thank them, and Dee came up with a suggestion.

''Mollie, if you could get someone to do the actual cooking, I'd be glad to plan the meals and buying for Indian Prairie.''

''You're feeling up to it?'' Mollie asked.

''Definitely!'' Dee assured her. ''I've been going crazy lying around here with nothing to do but boss Ray!''

''Take her up on it, Mollie,'' a laughing Ray requested. ''Please!''

''But who am I going to get?'' Mollie mused.

''What about U-Bear?'' Dee suggested. ''He used to work in that Chicago hashhouse. Maybe he'd fill in?''

Mollie considered. ''It's an idea. And I've kind of missed his music.''

At home, she called Hubert. Yes, he was willing.

Finally, on Saturday, just as the hot weather broke, the electricity was restored. Mollie spent the day on the phone assuring the next week's guests that Indian Prairie was up and running once more.

Mollie breathed a sigh of relief—and plunged once more into full days as manager of a going concern. But for how long? The plan had been that when the family trade diminished with the starting of school,

Indian Prairie Farm would cater to weekend hunting parties, then close January through March. Was that going to be?

And the guesthouse renovation, which normally would be done in the fine fall weather—was that to be? And the battery-powered generator Ray suggested Mollie buy in case of any more blackouts—there was no sense in putting money into it if Indian Prairie was going to fold.

Yet there was still enough awkwardness between her and Sloan that Mollie kept putting off a conference. For one thing, she was very busy. For another, Sloan, now freed from horse-care duties, spent long hours either at Kish's dig site, or in his fifth-wheeler—helping him with his manuscript, so she said.

"I'm good at editing," she said when Mollie met her crossing the farmyard with a sheaf of papers under her arm. "The more time Kishko spends digging, the sooner he'll get out of here," she finished defensively at Mollie's smile.

You doth protest too much, Mollie thought.

August rushed to a close. Labor Day came and with it the end of the Indian Prairie family season. Mollie was at the dining-room table working on a balance sheet when Sloan entered the room. "Yes?"

"I need to talk to you, Mollie, about the farm."

Mollie felt a nervous rush; was the shoe about to drop?

"How are things going?" Sloan asked, nodding toward the balance sheet.

"Close."

Sloan looked around, seemingly not sure how to proceed. Finally she blurted, "I'll be twenty-one next month, you know."

"Yes?"

"I've decided to keep Indian Prairie Farm as it is now."

Mollie's heart lightened. She turned in her chair to face Sloan. "I'm glad. Your father would be so pleased—"

"I'm not doing it primarily for him," Sloan said with a frown. "But Kish is finding a few things at the dig—bits of pottery and so forth—that make him think he may be onto something. He says the farm, as it's used now, poses little threat to his site. As long as somebody responsible is in charge of it."

Mollie waited for Sloan to fire her.

Sloan cleared her throat. "Kish has so many duties that will take him away from the site. He thinks that you and Zach are the only two he can trust to respect it. To see that it's never exploited."

"But Zach is gone—"

"Yes. But Kish is sure that Zach will eventually answer the call of his blood. Meanwhile, we want you to continue as manager."

Mollie rose slowly. "Why? If you want Zach to return—" She shook her head. "He won't, as long as I'm here."

"Maybe not."

"And then you're stuck with just me."

The faintest color came up in Sloan's tanned cheeks. "I'm beginning to see the value of Kish's work. I want to help with it any way I can. So, if it makes him more comfortable leaving you in charge here, I agree."

Mollie was too surprised to give an immediate answer. "Let me think about it," she said.

Sloan nodded her assent and left.

Mollie began to pace. This should have been a happy moment for her. Indian Prairie was saved, and so was her "dream job." Except it wasn't a dream job anymore, now that Zach was gone—

The phone interrupted. If only it would be Zach—

"Hello? Oh—Aunt Gwen."

"Don't be disappointed. Have you heard from him?"

"No. I don't expect to."

"Mollie." Aunt Gwen's tone was kindly, but resigned. Tired. "I'm sorry I haven't called you since . . . uh, well, you know when. I've been doing a lot of thinking. And wishing. That I'd done things differently. That I'd never caused you or anyone else pain. Henry's dream—I've made a botch of it."

"That's not certain." Mollie proceeded to tell her aunt about the conference she'd just had with Sloan.

"Mollie, is it just possible that the farm has accomplished for Sloan at least part of what Henry hoped it would? I mean, this James Kishko Kincannon has obviously gotten Sloan interested in something outside herself."

"It's possible," Mollie affirmed.

"But what kind of man is Kish?"

Mollie smiled to herself. "Different. But good. And no fortune hunter. And he calls Sloan 'dear one.' "

" 'Dear one?' " Aunt Gwen gasped. "Has she had a complete personality change?"

"Well, I think it's more a development of something that was always there."

Aunt Gwen seemed to ponder a moment. "At any rate, Sloan needs to meet with me and the estate lawyer in Chicago. October is fast approaching. Would you give her that message?"

"Of course, Aunt Gwen."

"Mollie." Aunt Gwen's voice went very soft, with a catch. "I love you, just as I always have. I hope you can forgive me."

"That happened before you'd left the farm, Aunt Gwen. I'm learning—the hard way—just how much you can love a man. How much you'd do to honor him."

"Mollie, all I've ever wanted for you—for all of us—is good. But maybe Zach told the terrible truth. Maybe I do feel guilty. Do you think that if I admitted that to Zach—?"

"Aunt Gwen, I'm not sure you or I can say anything now to make Zach feel better toward us. But what about Sloan? Maybe she's the one you should be telling."

Aunt Gwen sighed. "I'll think about it, Mollie. Just ask her to come to Chicago as soon as she can."

Half an hour later, Mollie and Star approached the dig site in the Outback. Kish and Sloan were standing close together, examining a small object in Kish's hand.

"It's a gunflint," Kish said, holding the object toward Mollie. "Used to strike fire to the powder in early guns. This is spall-type, made by European flint knappers—and Native Americans—prior to 1740. Several of these were found at the Grand Village of the Kickapoo."

"Good work!" Mollie said.

Kish glanced at the dusty, grimy-handed girl at his side, praise in his eyes. "Sloan found it."

Sloan's smile was shy. Mollie wondered if she'd ever before been lauded for anything except her youth and beauty.

Mollie gave Sloan Aunt Gwen's message.

"I don't want to go to Chicago!" Sloan said, grimacing. "I want to stay here and work."

"But I'll be gone next week, dear one," Kish said. "A four-day seminar on 'Mound Builders of the Middle Mississippian Era' at the University of Illinois—I'm the guest lecturer. And then the opening of the new Mesoamerican ceramics display at Field Museum in Chicago. If you were visiting your stepmother, you could be there with me."

Sloan hesitated. Her distaste for meeting with Aunt Gwen was palpable. But at Kish's smile and nod, she said, "Oh. Well, I'll go to the house and make arrangements."

A strong, wistful certainty swept Mollie: *These people are in love! I wonder—do they realize it yet?*

Mounted on Shalimar for the ride back with Mollie, Sloan took time to gaze admiringly at Kish's muscular form, now reattached to a spade. "Bodmer," she whispered to Mollie, never taking her eyes off Kish. "Charles Bodmer did those wonderful portraits of Native Americans—fierce, dangerous men with Greek-god bodies, and eyes like smoldering coals! He could have been painting Kishko."

He could have been painting Zach, Mollie thought as she turned Star toward the house.

All the way across the broad meadows, through the dark, cool patches of timber, along the sparkling lakes, Mollie thought of Zach. How he loved Indian Prairie; how he had found his "dream job" here; how he had offered her the love of a lifetime—and she had ruined it all for him. For him? For both of them.

Sloan, as usual, said little, but her face glowed with whatever was passing through her thoughts.

As the ponies trotted into the farmyard, Mollie came to a decision. ''Sloan,'' she said, as the girl swung out of her saddle, ''while you're in Chicago, would you do something for me? Actually, for all of us?''

Sloan regarded her curiously. ''What?''

''Would you look up Zach and tell him—'' Mollie broke off until she could stop the tears that wanted to flow. ''Tell him I want him to come back to Indian Prairie. As manager.''

Sloan's surprise showed in her lifted brows. ''You'd work for him?''

Mollie shook her head no. ''I'd leave. I'm sure it's the only way he'd agree to come back.''

''But I thought this place was so important to you.''

''It is. But I know that if only one of us can be here, it should be Zach. He deserves it.''

Sloan was slow in answering. ''I'll see him. But Kish and I both know it was the combination of you and Zach that got this place off the ground.''

Now the tears were stinging Mollie's eyes. ''Thanks, Sloan. I know that, too. But I blew it.''

She wheeled Star; followed by ghosts of what might have been, Mollie rode like the wind toward the prairie.

Chapter Nineteen

"Mollie—what are you doing?"

Mollie turned from the box she was filling with books and personal papers stored in the dining-room closet. "Dee!" Her tired face creased in a smile. "It's so good to see you out!"

Dee pulled out a chair and sat at the table. "It's good to be out, Mol. Eight weeks as a semi-invalid is seven more than I can stand. But I repeat: What are *you* doing?"

Mollie dropped the last book into the box. "I'm pulling up stakes."

Dee looked startled. "Pulling up? Mollie, why?"

"I feel like I've made a mess of things here," Mollie said in a low voice. "Oh, not in running the place or balancing the budget," she hurried on over Dee's protest. "Just . . . other ways."

Dee rose and came slowly to Mollie's side. "I don't know what happened between you and Zach, but that's the problem, isn't it, Mollie?"

Mollie nodded. "Part of it." She sighed. "I can't go into detail. But in a course on human relations, I'd be lucky to rate a D."

"In a pig's eye!"

Mollie couldn't help a short laugh at Dee's expression.

''Thanks for the vote of confidence, Dee. But I'm moving on.''

''Is it that little snipe, Sloan?''

''No. Believe it or not, she's mellowing. I think she's in love—''

''With herself? I guarantee it!''

Mollie smiled again. ''No. With Kish. And he's in love with her.''

''Well, knock me over!''

''Yeah. That's kind of the way it struck me, too. But I think it's going to be a good thing.''

Dee opened her mouth to say more, but Mollie cut her off with a quick question about Dee's pregnancy. Mollie didn't want to explain any more about her situation. She'd waited a week before Sloan called from Chicago to say she'd talked to Zach. But Sloan had seemed evasive when Mollie tried to pin her down as to what he'd said. Now Mollie was convinced that one way or another, she was in her last days at Indian Prairie.

''. . . And all those cold winter days Ray will be inside, turning our spare bedroom into a nursery,'' Dee crooned happily. ''He's just as excited as I am! But we're having trouble deciding on names. . . .''

It was easy to keep Dee talking about Baby-Jones-to-Be.

Later, as Mollie walked Dee out to her car, Dee stopped.

''Hey—I don't hear zydeco.''

''Another big surprise—U-Bear has gone professional. When he found out the farm really doesn't need a cook for the winter months, he got a gig playing weekends in a Rock Island night spot.''

''Super! Mollie, honey.'' Dee put a kind hand on

Mollie's forearm. "Indian Prairie has been good for a lot of people. Before it's all over, I'll bet it'll be just as good for you."

"Thanks, Dee," Mollie said with an appreciative smile. "I hope so."

But as Dee drove down the lane, obviously so full of hope and joy for her own future, Mollie felt the greatest loneliness of her life. Sloan and Kish had found each other; Dee and Ray already had a strong, beautiful marriage going. Aunt Gwen? As much as she'd loved Uncle Henry, how long would it be before she found another husband? She always did. And then there was Mollie . . .

Mollie sighed and walked to the horse pasture gate. A doleful Junior met her gaze, chewing morosely at the drying autumn grass.

"Come here, boy," Mollie coaxed. "You've been moping ever since Zach left, haven't you?" she murmured as the horse plodded toward her. She scratched his forehead and let out another sigh. Long winter days—and longer winter nights. Alone.

"Well, boy," Mollie murmured, "that makes two of us."

It was early to feed the horses, but Mollie needed activity. She went into the barn and began measuring feed. Once the herd was whistled in, she started at the far end with Junior and moved down the line, currying, petting, hugging each steed in turn. "I'm going to miss you guys so much!" she whispered, arms around Pet's neck.

She heard a squeak of brakes. Glancing out the barn door, she saw Kish's old truck pulling to a stop in the farmyard. At least she wouldn't be the only human on the place tonight.

Suddenly Junior's head jerked out of his oats. He began to dance, and his eyes rolled with his long, high neigh.

"What's wrong, Junior?" Mollie went to his side to try to settle him. Junior wasn't to be settled. In the interests of her own safety, Mollie dodged back out of his space.

"Need some help?"

Mollie froze at the soft, warm, Chicagoese voice. Her heart leaped even as she spun toward the door. Zach stood there. He smiled, yet his eyes were black as night. Was it with anger? Or some other emotion?

Junior let out another ear-splitting scream and tried to break loose from his rope.

"Hey, you big galoot." Zach came straight to Junior's space and shoved in beside him. "Are you tryin' to say you missed me?"

Junior nuzzled at Zach's chest, then calmed as Zach ran a soothing hand over his withers. The high-pitched neighs turned into low, rumbling nickers.

"He's been down ever since you left, Zach," Mollie said over the huge lump in her throat.

Zach turned slowly to Mollie. His high-cheekboned face, his beautiful dark eyes—Mollie tried desperately to read in them what he felt.

And then he spoke. Softly. "I've been down, too, Mollie. How about you?"

Mollie could barely speak, what with the ups and downs of her heart. "Oh, Zach, I've been in the pits!" she finally managed.

There was an awkward silence. Mollie didn't know what to say—what to think.

"Mollie, I'm sorry—"

"Zach, I was wrong—"

The apologies tumbled on top of one another. There was another painful silence as a thousand questions crashed through Mollie's brain. Suddenly Zach kicked over a feed bucket as he lurched to pull Mollie into his arms.

"Baby, baby, baby!" he whispered into Mollie's hair. "I've been such a fool! Can you let me back into your life?"

"You've never been out of it, Zach!" Mollie cried over a heart bursting with joy.

For a while, there was no talk, just long, beautiful kisses and clinging, as if they'd just stepped back from a horrible free fall.

Then Mollie began a torrent of "sorries," staunched by Zach's finger pressed tenderly against her mouth. "Shh, shh!" he murmured. "If you were wrong, so was I. If I'd heard you out—if I hadn't been so crazy with hurt—I wouldn't have spent the past few weeks wondering how to get out of the hole I dug for myself."

"There's blame enough to go around for a whole bunch of us, Zach."

He nodded yes. "So I've been told."

Mollie looked up at him, questioning.

"First by your aunt, then by Sloan."

Mollie pulled back in surprise.

"It seems the two of them have come to some kind of truce. They both agree Indian Prairie should live— even if they want it for different reasons. Anyway, Gwen called Sloan and me in to apologize. To both of us." He chuckled ruefully. "Of course, being Gwen, she couldn't let go before she'd clobbered me for giving up a slab of my life to help a relative, then cutting you dead for doing the same thing."

"Zach, I told her not to say anything—"

"But she was right. When Sloan filled me in on the rough time you'd pulled through here—when she said you'd give up your 'dream job' so I could have it—" Zach cradled Mollie's face in a tender hand. "Mollie, all I could think was, 'This sacrifice—the job, the place she loves—it comes out of the same big heart that couldn't turn away her aunt. And I deserve to be kicked!' "

"No, Zach. You deserve to run this place. You've made it the success it is."

"*We've* made it the success it is," Zach gently contradicted. " 'Manager' is just a word. Makes no difference what you call either of us, we're a team— aren't we, Mollie?"

Mollie let out a long, happy breath. "Yes! Oh, yes!"

The sun was going down by the time the two could let go of each other and head for the house. At sight of Kish's truck, Mollie stopped. "How come you're in the truck, instead of on the Harley?"

"Long story, baby. The highlights are, number one: Kish is coming back to Indian Prairie with Sloan. And two: I've sold the Harley to Todd Wingate. He wanted it bad."

"But Zach, it meant so much to you!"

"Honey, what's a guy with a wife and kids and mortgage need of a motorcycle? That *is* what I'm going to be, isn't it?"

Mollie's reply was instant and joyous. "Street boy— just you try to get out of it!"

The wind rushed against Mollie's face, leaving her almost breathless. She leaned into Zach's shoulders, warm and powerful beneath his silky white shirt. Her ankle-length wedding gown whipped like froth as the Harley took another curve.

The crest of a hill, a swooping circle, and the Harley stopped at the highest point of Indian Prairie. For a second, the riders stayed motionless, catching their breath. Then Zach dismounted and lifted Mollie off.

"Zach," Mollie whispered close to his ear. "When you said you had some wedding surprises for me, I never dreamed riding the Harley out here would be one of them. How'd you convince Todd to let you borrow it?"

"Easy. I told him you'd like it. He still wants to impress you, honey."

Zach let her feet reach the ground, but Mollie's arms stayed wrapped around his neck. Far off, revelry—and zydeco—sounded from the Shallows, where a wedding reception still partied on.

"I've got another little surprise for you, baby," Zach murmured, unwrapping from Mollie long enough to fetch a paper from the Harley saddlebag. He put it in Mollie's hands. "This is my wedding gift to you."

Mystified, Mollie held the paper up to the full October moon. "It looks like some kind of—legal paper, Zach."

"You know Sloan was twenty-one last week? This is the deed we've been working on since she came to Chicago. She's sold me the guesthouse and forty acres around it. And we have first option to buy more acreage when we can swing it."

Mollie was speechless. She started to tremble with excitement. "Zach," she finally managed, "we'll own part of Indian Prairie? How . . . where did you get the money—?"

Zach laughed softly. ''The bike. You know your aunt said Henry took it in from a down-and-out actor? Well, Todd did some research. When he found out it was once owned by Ward Jason, the big gun in Hollywood—you know Wingate—price was no object!''

''Oh, Zach! This is more than I've ever dared hope for—'' Mollie broke off to kiss her new husband soundly. Then: ''This *is* what you really want?''

''This is *everything* I want! *You*—and Indian Prairie.''

In the magic of a golden moon, whispering trees, an almost mystical calling of land and blood, Zach turned Mollie to the very place where he had first uttered the wonderful words: ''I love you!'' Through the light and shadow, she saw the outlines of a wickiup, a true Native-American bark lodge.

''My last surprise, Mollie,'' Zach whispered, drawing her close. ''This is a wedding present from Kish. Come on, take a look.''

Inside the wickiup, soft, clean blankets covered the thick grass—and an air mattress. Along the rough walls stood a Native American water jar, and a few L. L. Bean–type camp comforts.

Zach took Mollie into his arms; she twined her fingers in the rich, dark hair blowing softly around his handsome face. She gloried in the wild beat of his heart next to hers.

''Tomorrow,'' Zach murmured, ''we start a nice, civilized honeymoon in Chicago. But tonight—''

He drew himself to his full, powerful height. His soft tone turned regal, his face went Kish-proud. But laughter—and love—danced in his warm black eyes. ''Tonight it is midnight on the prairie. Tonight, beautiful farm girl—*I am Kickapoo!*''

Mollie's joy spilled in radiant laughter. ''Tonight, beloved street boy—*I am glad!*''